"When are we going out together?"

"There you go."

"I want to see you again, Ted, and not to talk about dogs. I want you to meet my friends."

"Do they hang out in salad bars?"

"No, those are Delphine's friends. A lot of her friends are the same as mine, and a lot are different."

"Sounds like you're loaded with friends."

"I'm popular. Can't help it. So how about tonight? There's a party a few streets away. We can walk. No mother, no automobile. Say yes."

She was beautiful, she was begging me, and nothing else seemed to be important. What Mia had told me fizzled, what Laura advised me fizzled too. I had the feeling of victory again, the same feeling I had at the party the first night in Dallas. What were a few doubts compared to the reality of a beautiful, begging Beth Ann Deering. You believe what you want to believe.

MARJORIE SHARMAT is the author of nearly a hundred books, including *How to Meet a Gorgeous Guy, How to Meet a Gorgeous Girl, How to Have a Gorgeous Wedding, I Saw Him First, He Noticed I'm Alive . . . And Other Hopeful Signs,* and *Two Guys Noticed Me . . . And Other Miracles,* all available in Dell Laurel-Leaf editions. She lives with her husband in Tucson, Arizona.

ALSO AVAILABLE IN LAUREL-LEAF BOOKS:

Are We There Yet?

Marjorie Sharmat

Published by
Dell Publishing
a division of
Bantam Doubleday Dell Publishing Group, Inc.
666 Fifth Avenue
New York, New York 10103

This work was first published in the U.S.A. in 1985 by Pacer Books, a member of The Putnam & Grosset Group under the pseudonym Wendy Andrews.

ISBN: 0-440-20680-4

RL: 5.1

Published by arrangement with the author

Printed in the United States of America

August 1990

10 9 8 7 6 5 4 3 2 1

OPM

To Beverly, for guiding me through these travels

Are We There Yet?

1

I used to know more about cars than I knew about girls, but now I think my knowledge of both subjects is about even. I don't plan to write the Ted Fisher User's Manual on Girls, but I know that if I decided to do it, I could do a good job. I picked up a real education on vacation in Dallas, Texas.

I had always heard that Texas has the biggest and the best, but I never believed it. Then I met two girls, one incredible and one semi-incredible, and they seemed to like me right away. Both of them. I was surprised. Let's face it, I was overwhelmed.

Like any guy, I like attention. But it's not usual that I get it. On the trip from my house in Phoenix, Arizona, to my aunt and uncle's house in Dallas, I was stuck in the back seat of a car with my older sister, Mia, who managed to get herself a boyfriend along the way, and my younger sister, Heidi, who more or less ate and swam her way from Phoenix to Dallas.

Since boys are Mia's big thing, and swimming and eating are Heidi's, and this trip was our parents' idea, where did that leave *me*, Ted Fisher? As a loser, that's where it left me. Sometimes at home in Phoenix I felt like a loser. But now I was one across state lines, oozing, spreading.

I had spent depressing hours by a pool in New Mexico trying to pick up a girl who didn't want to get picked up—at least not by me. Then I met this disgustingly rich girl Cecile Trumbull, who must have been studying to be a nymphomaniac, only she didn't need any lessons. Good thing I could run faster than she could. Then I met this guy who was a real sleaze, and he was going to introduce me to some great girls. But the great girls were dressed in green sequins and pink leather body suits and fishnet stockings. They were also old enough to be my mother. Finally we stopped at a ranch where my luck improved—or so I thought. Beth Ann Wagner came into my life. She was gorgeous, but she was fickle. Halfway through our date she left me for a guy with handmade cowboy boots and a fat genuine-leather wallet. She especially liked the wallet and its fatness.

Should I mention the evening I spent playing cards with an elderly lady and a ten-year-old boy? I lost.

My male ego had been pummeled throughout the Southwest by the time we arrived at Aunt Jewel and Uncle Tony's huge house in Dallas. I was in a state of private collapse as we drove up their driveway. But when I saw their house, I snapped back. It was *really* big. They must have turned rich. I hoped they hadn't turned obnoxious. I loved my aunt and uncle. They didn't have any kids of their own, and whenever we got together, they spoiled Mia, Heidi and me like crazy. You might say they temporarily adopted us. We became their kids. My parents were glad to lend us out this way, because Tony and Jewel seemed to need to be somebody's parents.

The last time I saw them was in their run-down apartment in Pittsburgh, Pennsylvania. Now they were standing waiting for us in front of this huge house. They were wearing boots. This should have clued me to the fact that they had left Pittsburgh way behind. Aunt Jewel is very short, like Mom, and Uncle Tony is very tall, like John Wayne. When you see them together, you get the feeling that he once must have rescued her from something and that they stayed together as rescuer and rescuee. He loomed over her like a guardian.

There were so many hugs and kisses going around that Heidi kissed me by mistake. She said to Uncle Tony, "Don't crush me." She had a point. He looked like an invincible, grim-jawed, Western legend. I wondered if his neighbors knew he came from Pittsburgh.

After the hugs-and-kisses session and the "Did you have a good trip?" question-and-answer session, Uncle Tony said, "We're having a barbecue tonight. We want you to meet all our neighbors and friends."

"Food!" said Heidi. "Great!"

"So soon?" said Mom.

Mom was tired from the trip. My father was tired, too. Mia just wanted to lie around and dream about her new boyfriend, Neal Guest. And I wasn't interested in meeting friends of my aunt and uncle.

But Jewel and Tony took their cue from Heidi. "We knew you'd be pleased," said Jewel.

We didn't even have time to unpack before the party started.

The party was held around the swimming pool in their enormous backyard. The yard looked more like a national park. Aunt Jewel and Uncle Tony must have invited everyone they ever met. People kept coming. Food kept coming. Every steak in Dallas must have been at that party. If you didn't like steak, there were, in addition, enchiladas, tacos, flautas, rellenos, tostadas, chimichangas. Some of these were stuffed with shrimp, cod, crab, cheeses, sour cream, chicken, shredded lettuce and beans. I know about the stuffings, because I picked apart some of the food while I was trying to figure out what was inside. You never knew what combinations were being used, and when I finally discovered something that merely had chicken, refried beans, and shredded lettuce, I stuck with it.

Most of the guests were middle-aged, dressed in casual clothes like denim jeans with diamonds sticking out of the pockets. Actually I'm exaggerating, but if you put two people side by side who are both wearing jeans, one person might look wealthy and the other might look poverty-stricken. You get vibes that one of them is dressed in an expensive costume, and the other is dressed in his one and only pair of pants. I figured that everyone here had closets bulging with clothes. Except my family. We weren't poor, but we definitely weren't Texas rich.

People were friendly, and I got hugs and kisses, smears of sour cream and refried beans on my face and shirt. Can people really like you so much when they don't even know you?

Then I noticed two girls eyeing me. They looked older than Heidi, who's eleven, and younger than Mia, who's seventeen. I'm fifteen, and they looked a little younger than me. Fourteen? They were eating while they were staring. I wouldn't have complained if they smeared their melted cheese and guacamole over me.

One of the girls had bright-blond hair, and the other was a brunette. The blond was beautiful. The brunette was spectacular. They started to walk toward me. I looked over my shoulder. Toward *me!* The two of them were heading straight toward Ted Fisher, the one who had spent almost a week traveling in the disasterland of crushed hopes and raw rejection. In the minute it took for them to reach me, a new Ted Fisher was born.

2

The girl with the bright-blond hair asked, "Are you Ted?"

Was I already famous in Dallas? Famous with this beautiful blond creature? Was I dreaming?

The spectacular dark-haired girl added, "Of course he's Ted. Can't you tell?"

This made me wonder what my distinguishing marks and characteristics were. I decided not to ask.

"Welcome to Dallas," said the blond girl. "We both live down the street. I'm Delphine Rasmussen and this is my friend Beth Ann Deering."

Beth Ann? Not another girl named Beth Ann! Did they raise Beth Anns wholesale, like cattle, in this part of the Southwest? Or were they more like oil wells? Beth Ann Wagner had left me high and dry at that ranch in New Mexico after gushing all over the place when she first met me.

"Beth Ann?" I repeated. "I guess one Beth Ann isn't

related to another Beth Ann because they only have the same *first* name, and that doesn't count."

Beth Ann Deering seemed puzzled. I was off to a bad start.

I went on. "Actually the name Beth Ann has a very pleasant association for me. I know one."

"Yeah?" Beth Ann was all smiles.

"I met Beth Ann on my trip from Phoenix to here. Actually I'm trying to recover from that trip. There's plenty to recover from."

Delphine raised her eyebrows. "Really? Like what? Tell me, Ted. I'm a great listener."

"So am I," said Beth Ann. "Don't leave out *anything*. I love to hear about vacations. Especially the kind that one has to recover from."

"Definitely that kind," said Delphine.

What could I say? I couldn't tell them the truth. I knew for a fact that beautiful girls aren't impressed by failure. I looked around. I was in Texas. Everything was bigger than life. I was at an excessive party. The food was excessive. The guests were excessive. But Ted Fisher? He was not excessive; he was in danger of becoming invisible. I would only be staying in Dallas for a week or so.

I cast aside the old Ted Fisher.

"You think there's money in Dallas? You think there are beautiful women in Dallas?" I started. "You think there are mansions in Dallas? You should see Arizona. You should see New Mexico. You should have been where I've been."

"Where?" Delphine asked. "I love a man who's been around."

15

"Me, too," said Beth Ann. "What happened on your trip?"

"I'm not the kind of guy who talks about things like that," I said.

"You're a real gentleman," said Beth Ann. "Keeping quiet and everything. But you can tell me. I'd love to share your experiences, Ted."

"You've got *me* hooked," Delphine said. "It's such an interesting story."

"I haven't told it yet."

"I know that. But the *potential* is so interesting. Like, going from state to state. It's a personal travelogue." Delphine gave me a dimpled smile.

"That's exactly how I was going to describe it," said Beth Ann.

"I'll get you something to drink, so your throat won't get dry," Delphine offered. She started to walk off.

"No, I'll go," said Beth Ann. "What kind of soda would you like, Ted?"

"Anything," I said.

They *both* went to get me some soda. I loved Dallas!

I watched them as they walked over to a table. They seemed in a hurry. I hoped they would take their time. What would I say to them when they got back? I felt like I was on stage, but nobody had told me what lines to say.

"All alone, Ted?" Tony came up to me.

"Not exactly."

"You've got to get into the spirit of things, Ted."

Tony gave me a pat on the head. Then he reached up and took off his enormous cowboy hat and put it on my head. "This will make you feel like a real Texan. Try it on for size."

It was much too big. I could feel that it was.

"Your head will grow into it if you stay in Dallas long enough," Tony said, and he walked off, leaving me wearing his hat. I wished I knew what I looked like in it. But having it on my head gave me a surge of confidence.

When Delphine and Beth Ann came back, each with a glass of soda in her hand, I was ready for them. They didn't mention the hat. They just waited for me to continue my story. I sipped some soda and said, "Well, I met this rich girl—a real millionairess—who lived in this incredible mansion and she was so crazy about me that I could hardly get away from her."

This was true. No need to mention that Cecile Trumbull was not fussy about whom she grabbed or that her grabbing made me nervous.

"What did you do?" Delphine asked.

"Do? I told her she couldn't have everything she wanted. I lectured her about compromise. When I left Cecile—that was her name—she was a wiser, more compassionate, more understanding human being."

Beth Ann looked at me with what I would call awe. "Was it hard? How much time did you have to turn her into this wiser, more compassionate, more understanding human being?"

"Just a couple of hours."

"Was that the high point of your trip?"

"Oh no. I'm not there yet. Turning this rich girl's life and values around, well, that was important, of course. But then I met a guy who begged me to go to

17

this party he was throwing. And he had all these fabulous girls who were, well, extremely anxious to meet me."

"The guy begged you?" said Delphine. "What was he like?"

"In what way were the girls he wanted to introduce you to fabulous?" asked Beth Ann.

How could I answer with complete honesty? True, I had left that sleazy guy's party the minute I walked in, but telling them that would not make the right impression on Delphine and Beth Ann.

"The guy and the girls were movie stars and TV personalities," I explained. "I can't reveal their names. They were on location at the motel where I was staying. They were making a major film."

"Was that the most interesting part of your trip?" asked Delphine. "Are we there yet?"

"No, we're not there yet. The best part was when I met this girl Beth Ann at a ranch."

"That I'd really like to hear about," said Beth Ann. "People named Beth Ann are usually interesting. What happened?"

I was getting in deeper. "Are you ready for this?" I asked.

Both girls nodded.

"This Beth Ann was older than me. I mean I'm eighteen. I look younger but I'm eighteen. Well, she was old. Maybe twenty-five. Very experienced. Really knew men. And she asked me to *marry* her! I'd only known her for a few hours."

Delphine and Beth Ann looked shocked. Did they believe me? I hadn't meant to go this far. I hadn't

18

meant to lie about my age. I was fifteen, and I looked fifteen. But I knew I was scoring with these girls. It felt wonderful—a little scary, but great. How long could I go on with it? I had never done anything like this before. Once in a while I exaggerate a little, but that's normal. Now I was caught up in a story that was beginning to resemble a Russian novel or a soap opera on TV.

Delphine asked, "Did you accept?"

"Accept what?" I snapped out of my reverie. "Oh, the marriage proposal. Of course not. But I let her down gently. I told her if she knew me long enough she'd find that I had a flaw or two. Nothing serious, but still, I wasn't perfection and I wanted her to know that."

"I love modesty," said Beth Ann. "Isn't he modest?"

"He sure is," said Delphine.

They were talking about me.

Beth Ann kept on. "It's not a common trait. It's getting more and more rare. You hardly find it at all in men in Texas."

"We need more of it," said Delphine. She turned back to me. "So that was your trip, Ted? That was the best part?"

"No."

"You mean we're not there yet?" asked Beth Ann. "You told us that was the best part."

"I forgot something."

"Go on."

"First I think I need an enchilada."

"You deserve it after all you've been through," said Delphine.

These girls were fantastic. They believed me. They admired me. Ted Fisher's adventures were a big hit. After I got my enchilada, I'd have to continue my story. But it was getting harder and harder. How did I get into this? I knew. My ego. All around me at this party I heard the buzzing of success. I heard mink. I heard cattle. I heard Neiman-Marcus. I heard oil wells. I heard a guy say, "Ted!"

My fame was spreading. A guy I instantly wished I looked like put his hand on my shoulder. Taco shoulder now. These Texans were messy. Then the guy shook my hand. "I'm Randy Haliday and I live next door to your aunt and uncle. Hello, and welcome to Dallas."

Randy was a rugged-looking fellow, very tall and definitely on his way to helping keep the legends of Texas men alive. I sensed he could be competition. Especially when I saw Beth Ann's eyes fastened on him.

Randy Haliday didn't need to tell tall tales. He was tall enough without them. Suddenly I wondered how much I could ever really like Dallas.

3

Randy got shorter. He sat down on the ground after he got a steak. He looked like a steak person. Actually, he looked more like he could eat half a cow and it would all turn to muscle. But as I stared at him I realized he was a lot older than me. In his twenties, probably. Too old for these girls—I hoped.

"Your aunt and uncle said we had a lot in common," he said.

It should only have been true. I, at age fifteen, showed no signs of growing into someone virile. Some girls back home liked my dark eyes and my skinny frame and my superior knowledge of cars. But that was in Phoenix, where I didn't have to worry about first impressions. When Ted Fisher hit the road on this trip he traveled straight to Zero Junction. Randy Haliday was the final nail in my coffin. Without him I figured I might have had a chance with Delphine or Beth Ann.

The girls started to talk to Randy. And joke and laugh with him. They were talking like old friends, like they had all been pals since childhood. Then I realized that they were. Randy was not a novelty to Delphine and Beth Ann. He was old stuff. He may have been movie-star material but *I* was *new!* I had something going for *me*. I had materialized in this warm Texas night like a mystic cowboy.

"Ted was just telling us about his trip," Delphine said to Randy. "He was just getting to the best part."

"Don't let me stop you," said Randy.

"There's plenty of time to finish," I said. "Right now I'd like to introduce the other Fishers." I yelled to Heidi, who was a few feet away. She was gulping down food. "Heidi, come here!"

Heidi, her mouth stuffed with food, came over. "This is my sister, Heidi," I said. "She's eleven years old and a great swimmer."

I hoped this would be the beginning of a conversation about swimming. Maybe the Olympics or child athletes. Anything to take the heat off me. I didn't feel like coming up with any more stories.

"I love to swim, too," said Beth Ann. "Heidi, you're invited to my pool. All the Fishers are." She smiled at me.

"When?" Heidi asked.

"Any time."

"Thanks."

Everybody was quiet. So much for swimming. I saw Mia at a distance. It was too noisy to call to her. She must have seen me with Randy, but she didn't come over. Since Mia had fallen in love with Neal

22

Guest, she had stopped paying attention to other guys. Mia had picked up Neal over a bottle of ketchup in a roadside restaurant outside of Tucson. I wouldn't recommend it as a way to meet somebody, but it worked for her. Now at seventeen, she considered herself old and wise as far as romance was concerned. She thought she knew everything. But I was sure I knew more about girls than she did. After all, in ten minutes I had two great-looking girls talking to me. Even when a local hunk came into the picture, I kept their attention. I was totally in charge of this situation. I was getting to be an expert without even trying.

Delphine pulled me aside.

"Secrets?" said Beth Ann. Then she gave me a little tug.

"One at a time," I said.

"I was first," said Delphine. She whispered to me. "Let's go to the movies some night, Ted."

"Sure," I said. "I'll call you."

Delphine slipped me her phone number. She must have had it prepared.

Beth Ann was watching us silently. I guess she gave up. Oh well, one date was enough.

But just as the party was breaking up, Beth Ann, eyelashes fluttering, caught my arm and asked, "How about coming to my house tomorrow night for a real Texas home-style dinner?"

"Sure honey." That's what they'd say in Texas, wouldn't they?

4

The last guest left at 2 A.M. By this time, Mom, Dad, Mia, Heidi and I were sitting around the pool, kind of beat. Tony and Jewel waved goodbye to somebody who could no longer see them, and joined us by the pool. Jewel was full of energy, as if she were just starting something, instead of finishing up. Tony seemed pleased about everything.

"Nice party, Jewel," he said, and he kissed her.

"It was great," Heidi said. "I've never been to anything like it."

"That's what I hoped," Jewel said. She sat down on a chair beside Mom. "We do things right in Texas."

"The best party ever," I said. I didn't say why. Two girls falling all over me. It was incredible. Now that the party was over, I had to analyze the situation. What had I done, what had I said to achieve such results? I was already forgetting the specific words. I had to write them down. I couldn't let them escape. It would be like losing diamonds.

I needed paper and pencil. I didn't have any.

"Jewel," I said, "could I borrow a pencil and some paper?"

"Of course. But what for at this unearthly hour?"

"I have to write a letter to a friend. I want to tell him about the party."

I think I was the friend.

"A letter?" Jewel put her hand on my mother's arm. "Who writes letters anymore?" Then she turned to me. "Darling, don't be ridiculous. We all send tapes around here. Nobody actually *writes*."

Mom was shocked. "You don't *write*?"

"Do you, Gwen? You and I have a telephone relationship. Verbal. That's where it's at these days." Jewel got up. "Ted dear, come with me. Your friend will love this."

"Doesn't his friend need something to play the tape on?" Mom asked. But Jewel was already walking into the house. I followed her. All I wanted was a simple pencil and a simple piece of paper, but this was Jewel's house, and she was operating on her own beam.

She went into the den and opened a desk drawer. She reached into the drawer. "Here," she said, "a micro-cassette. A tape recorder small enough to fit into your pocket. Batteries. A supply of tapes. You can talk to your friend forever."

Jewel started to press buttons. "Very simple. Play. Rewind. Pay attention."

"I know how to use it. A friend of mine has one

25

exactly like this. It cost a fortune. I mean this is expensive stuff, and a pencil and piece of paper will do fine."

"Ted, do you know how many of these recorders I have? Guess."

"Well—"

"Half a dozen at least. Why buy one of something when you can buy a dozen? Here. No arguments."

Jewel put the recorder in my hand. The minute she gave it to me I knew I was glad to have it. She was right. Talking was easier than writing. And faster. This little tape recorder was made for my situation.

"Thanks," I said. "I appreciate it."

"Nothing's too good for my nephew. Now you go to your room and write your letter while the ideas are still fresh."

She was a mind reader.

In my room I could hardly wait to confide in the tape recorder. I pushed the button to record. *"Tonight in Dallas, Texas, something incredible happened to me. I met two girls, Beth Ann and Delphine. I talked too much. I exaggerated like crazy. Actually I told some tall ones. And these girls loved it! How could they love it? I don't get it. I can't believe it worked. In Phoenix hardly anything worked. And nothing worked on this trip until tonight. What did I say? I can't remember. I've gone blank. I need this information for the future."*

I turned off the machine. I lay down on the bed. Suddenly the whole evening replayed itself in my head. I got up and told the tape recorder everything.

5

Uncle Tony kept apologizing to my family for being rich. He apologized for his many acres. He apologized for Venetia Villa, which was the name he and Aunt Jewel had given their house. He apologized for his Mercedes-Benz.

If he really felt guilty about his Mercedes-Benz, I could have relieved him of his guilt. I'm saving up to buy myself a wreck. I don't have my driver's license yet—only a learner's permit—but the minute I get my license I expect to have a wreck to drive. The Mercedes-Benz looked like a treasure beyond belief. I wanted it now and forever.

Although Uncle Tony and Aunt Jewel don't have any kids, they have a dog, Yums, whom they patted and hugged like he was a person. Uncle Tony was proud that this dog was not pedigreed, bought at a high price. He was a mutt that they got from the pound. Uncle Tony acted like this was a poverty-type gesture and that it wiped out wealth. He was still just a regular, nice guy who happened to be loaded.

I wondered what my parents were thinking about all of this. Mom and Jewel were close sisters, but Jewel had become rich and Mom hadn't. Mom and Dad are high-school teachers. Uncle Tony is some kind of real-estate tycoon, and Aunt Jewel is—well, she's his rich wife and that's it. Mom got envious, then disgusted with her rich friend Lizette Trumbull when we visited her on this trip. Maybe it's better not to leave home if you keep meeting people who are richer or sexier or smarter than you are. It makes you aware of all the depressing competition in the world, and even if you're not a competitive person, it can hurt.

The morning after the party we were all sitting around the table in the breakfast room, which had a big skylight and plants everywhere. I felt like I was in a greenhouse. A maid, whom Uncle Tony apologized for having—when she wasn't in earshot—served us breakfast.

"Did you all sleep well?" asked Aunt Jewel.

"Yes, Aunt Jewel," said Heidi.

"What's this 'Aunt Jewel' business? Sounds so formal," said Aunt Jewel. "We're just Tony and Jewel, no different from our Pittsburgh selves."

Aunt Jewel—*Jewel*—was trying to be plain like *Tony*. You'd have to be nuts to think they weren't rich. Unless everything was stolen.

"I hope you and Heidi don't mind sharing a guest room," Jewel said to Mia. "We have only three guest rooms."

28

"You've been to our house, Jewel—that's three more than we have at home," said Heidi.

Mom smiled. She seemed to have accepted Jewel and Tony's new wealth better than they had. She was happy for them. I think she felt sorry for Jewel deep down, because she never had kids. Money, even lots of money, wasn't as good as kids to Mom.

Tony dug his fork into his ham. "I had a terrible night," he said. "The Deerings' blasted dog's howling kept me up. Didn't you all hear him? What a racket!"

"No," Jewel answered for everybody.

"The Deerings," I said. "They live down the street or up the street, don't they? How could you hear their dog from here?"

"Sound carries in Texas," said Tony.

"Aren't they acres away?" asked Mia.

"Sound carries farther in Texas," Tony repeated. He turned to me. "How do you know the Deerings, Ted?"

"Beth Ann Deering was at your party last night."

"She was?"

Tony turned to Jewel. "You invited the Deerings?"

"Yes," said Jewel. "I didn't think you'd notice."

Imagine having a party so big that you can hope to hide some of your guests. I was impressed by this conversation.

"I didn't see them," said Tony. "Please don't invite them again, Jewel. Did they bring their dog?"

"Of course not, but they do live in the neighborhood. I admit that I'm not crazy about Mrs. Deering or Beth Ann, but she's Ted's age."

"Rock Deering is a jerk," Tony said, finishing up the Deering family.

29

"Rock?" I asked. "Who's that and is that his real name?"

"He claims it is," said Jewel. "It's Beth Ann's father."

I was going to dinner at the home of Rock Deering. It was beginning to sound not so great. "Beth Ann invited me there for dinner tonight," I said. "Why don't you like her, Jewel?"

Tony answered. "Go at your own risk."

"I'd really like to go," I said. "I mean I already said yes to Beth Ann."

Mia looked at me. Her face took on the wise-woman look. Just before we had reached Dallas, I confided in her about all the trouble I had with girls during the trip. Mia had said, "Dallas will be better." And she actually had squeezed my hand in a big-sister gesture she meant.

Heidi finished gulping down her breakfast. Then she said, "Mia met her boyfriend by borrowing a bottle of ketchup. Over food must be a great way to get boyfriends and girlfriends and stuff. Tony, don't you think that if a girl invites Ted for dinner, Ted should go?"

Mia's face turned red. Mine would have, but I don't blush.

Jewel asked, "You met a boyfriend over a bottle of ketchup, Mia?"

Mia was mad at Heidi. "Heidi spilled a bottle of ketchup over him, and I wiped it up!"

"But that—" Heidi started to say, but she stopped when she noticed Mia's face.

Heidi had to learn to keep her eleven-year-old mouth shut.

"Let's make some plans for our first day in Dallas." Mom changed the subject.

"I've already made them, Gwen," Jewel said as she poured her fifth cup of coffee. I didn't mean to count. It's just that I noticed she was probably a coffee addict. I don't think it's against the law though.

Jewel sipped. Then she said, "I've invited my club over this morning to meet you, Gwen. We're a cultural group. We're advancing the arts in Dallas. I'm giving this brunch in your honor."

"My honor?" Mom said. "Sounds so formal."

"They should be here in an hour."

"An hour? My honor? I'm hardly awake. And I've just had breakfast. Isn't it early?"

"We do a lot of eating in this city," said Jewel.

"Hooray for Dallas," said Heidi.

Mom looked like she wanted to go back to sleep. But Jewel was a planner. She had our vacation mapped out for us. I wondered if she left any time for just hanging around. I wondered how long Mom would put up with this. She knew her sister but never seemed prepared for these organized unasked-for activities.

"I want to see scenery," said Heidi. "And swimming pools."

"Not to worry," said Mia. "One of the girls we met last night, Delphine, offered to drive me around the city, and I'm sure she won't mind if you come. Is that okay?" Mia looked at Mom, Dad and Jewel as if she needed three permissions.

"Delphine Rasmussen," Jewel said. "She's not one of my favorite teens, but she'll probably make a good tour guide. That is, her mother will. Delphine owns the car, but her mother does the driving."

"Huh?" Delphine already owned a car! Cars, my passion, made Delphine even more appealing.

"Then again," said Jewel, "Randy would probably make a better guide. Know what I mean?" Jewel winked at Mia.

Mia knew what Jewel meant. "Randy seems nice," Mia replied, "but I really do have a boyfriend, and I'm loyal to him. You'd like him, Jewel. Mother likes him. Don't you, Mom?"

"Right, right," said Jewel as she smiled at my mother and poured her sixth cup of coffee. "A boy who likes ketchup."

I was curious about Delphine. "What's the matter with Delphine, Jewel?"

"She lacks sincerity—like her mother. If she's going to be a hypocrite, she should wait until she's thirty or forty and do it right."

Tony broke in. "She's okay. Her family's dog doesn't bark all night. In fact, they have a cat. What more could you want from a girl?"

"Tell him, Ted," said Heidi, who laughed as I gave her a look that said "shut up."

Jewel finished her last cup of coffee. "Go, Mia," she said, finally giving Mia an answer.

"Can I go, too?" asked Heidi.

"Of course," said Jewel.

"How about Ted?" asked Heidi.

"Fine," said Jewel.

We had a new mother.

My mother and father exchanged looks. But they let Jewel play mother. I didn't want to see Delphine with Mia and Heidi along as escorts. And Delphine's mother, too. Still, I wondered if Delphine had invited Mia to go sightseeing in the hope that I'd go along, too. Maybe Delphine was so anxious she couldn't wait for me to invite her to the movies. Delphine might suffer all day long. Then I smiled—suffering makes girls easier to get.

"Thanks, but no thanks," I said.

After breakfast Tony took Dad out to play golf. He had Dad's day planned, like Jewel had done for Mom. Mia and Heidi went to Delphine's house. Mom and Jewel went upstairs to get dressed for the brunch.

I went to my room. It was a great room. Parts of the walls were made of tile with designs in them, and the carpet looked like fur. It didn't look at all like a gym, but that was what I was about to use it for. I was going to do my daily exercises—an hour's worth. I'm building up my endurance, my muscles, my entire body. I tried to do my exercises while we were traveling, but I didn't have much room or time. Now I had plenty of catching up to do. Cramped in the back seat of that car next to my sisters probably stunted my growth. The physical arrangement in the car was me in back next to Mia who was next to Heidi. Mia hated being Mia-in-the-middle. My parents always sat in front. In spite of this cramped situation, I ended the trip to Dallas feeling closer in a mental sort of way to Mia and Heidi and my parents. The trip had brought us together in ways that just living under the same roof in Phoenix never could. I had to admit that it was kind of nice.

I took out my exercise book. I like this book because it doesn't have a picture of a movie star or TV star on it. Movie stars should stick to doing movies and not tell people how to exercise. I took off my clothes, put on my exercise shorts, and thought about the superior body I'd be presenting at Beth Ann's house tonight. I stretched out on the rug. The furry stuff tickled my back. I did thirty sit-ups, forty push-ups, and then I did my lifts. Arms, legs, chest. I was sweating. My body was starting to glisten. It would be great to transport the glisten to Beth Ann's house. Or maybe disgusting if she didn't go for glisten.

What *could* I transport to Beth Ann's house? Was I supposed to take a present? Like candy or flowers? Kibbles for her dog? I hadn't any idea. In Phoenix girls never asked me to an actual dinner at their houses. We just raided refrigerators.

I headed for the shower.

I heard the doorbell, or chimes, or Oriental gong, or whatever it was. Yums barked.

"Somebody answer!" Jewel yelled. "I'm dressing."

"Me, too," Mom yelled.

Where was the maid? I've heard about servants who are considered to be members of the household, but in this house it was the opposite. The maid appeared and disappeared and seemed not to belong anywhere. It was as if her job depended on her not being noticed or even having a name.

I stopped halfway to the shower. I listened. Was

anybody going to answer the door? It was up to me, the glistening doorman.

I went downstairs and opened the door. A woman who seemed overly enthusiastic was standing there.

"Hello," she said. "I'm Nancy Erskine-Chamberlin, and you must be one of the visiting Fishers. Ted, isn't it?"

"You've got it," I said.

"I'm so pleased to meet you. I'm a member of Jewel's club. Am I early for the brunch?"

I shrugged. "Want to come in?"

Of course she wanted to come in. What a dumb question to ask her. But I felt strange standing there with my shiny body. She reminded me of my mother's best friend.

Nancy Erskine-Chamberlin walked in and sat down on one of the living-room couches. She patted the seat beside her. "Come join me," she said, "while I wait for the others."

I wasn't dressed for sitting on a white living-room couch. I belonged in a shower. But the woman seemed to want me to join her. I sat down.

"You're a hunk," she said, smiling. "Your aunt didn't exaggerate."

6

I'm usually instantly responsive to the word *hunk*. I don't hear it often enough applied to me. But from this middle-aged lady! Was I multigenerational in my appeal?

"And a nice boy," she added. "Muscles, sweating skin, the gleam of youth. It's all over your body."

Nancy Erskine-Chamberlin was sitting there in a dull, tailored dress, her hair was plain, and I imagined that her house was dusted, proper and clean. She just didn't look like a hunk-oriented person. I was suspicious. My luck with females in Dallas was now more fantastic than I wanted it to be. Beth Ann and Delphine were about all I could handle in a week's time. I should never have answered the door in my exercise shorts.

I didn't know what to say to her. Nobody in my place, in my shorts, would know what to say to this lady. Fortunately I didn't have to think of anything.

She went on talking. "I have a beautiful daughter exactly your age and you two would make a perfect couple."

Daughters are always beautiful to their mothers.

She kept going. "Would you like to meet her?"

I'd like to check up on her, that's what I'd like to do. But I couldn't say that.

She was waiting for an answer. She didn't wait long. She said, "Do you feel on the spot? Don't you fret. I'll just work something out with your Aunt Jewel."

Over my dead glistening body she would. Blind dates were usually the pits. Not that I dated so much. But I knew from talk—and anyway, I had enough with two Texas beauties.

The maid reappeared and started fixing a table filled with wonderful-looking pastries and tea and coffee. Then Jewel walked into the room. Why hadn't one of them answered the door?

Jewel sniffed. I had to get to the shower. I said, "Excuse me," and I made my exit.

Upstairs I turned on the shower. Then I turned it off. I had something else to do first. I turned on my tape recorder. I spoke into it: *Glistening body attracts older women. Remember this for when you're older.*

After I showered and dressed, I heard conversation going on downstairs. Jewel's club members were talking and laughing and sometimes shrieking. I hoped Mom was having a good time. Mom isn't always comfortable around new people. She's quiet around most strangers. Maybe it has something to do with her being short and looking like a doll sitting on a shelf. That's a nutty way to describe her, but that's the way we think of Mom. It's amazing how much Jewel looks like her, but she wouldn't remind anyone of a doll. She projects. In private, with just her family and close friends, Mom projects, too. Or when she's angry even at strangers. She's capable of becoming a dynamo. During the earlier part of the vacation, when a noisy party broke out over our motel rooms and we were trying to get our rooms changed, Mom put up a fantastic fight with the motel manager. She intimidated him into changing our rooms!

Jewel's downstairs brunch reminded me of the noisy party at the motel. The women were getting louder. I wondered if there was a back door I could get out of without anyone seeing me. Six o'clock and my date were a long way off. I decided to see if Randy was around.

I put my tape recorder in my pocket. Maybe I'd pick up some useful hints about girls. Randy was older and probably experienced.

I knew that Randy lived next door, but right or left? I'd take a chance with left. I walked along the curving street. It was a magnificent street, but "next door" in Dallas wasn't my idea of next door. It was a hike. I rang the bell at what I hoped was Randy's house. Great luck, he answered the bell.

"Greetings," he said. "Ted, come on in."

Randy's house had a huge inside entrance and from what I could see, rooms to match. He invited me into the kitchen. "I was just having some lunch," he said. "Join me."

I saw a peanut-butter and jelly sandwich with one

bite out of it on the table. "Sorry, I didn't mean to barge in. Jewel went from breakfast to brunch and I guess I'm confused about time."

Randy sat down and pushed a loaf of bread and a jar of peanut butter and a jar of jelly toward me. I sat down and looked at them. "Don't you have tacos and stuff like that for lunch? Isn't this Texas?"

Randy smiled. "Sometimes. So, what are you up to today, anyway? How come you're not out on the town?"

I leaned across the table and took Randy's knife. I started to make a sandwich. "I could have seen the town, I guess. Delphine Rasmussen is taking Mia and Heidi around, and I could have gone."

"In one of the jazziest cars in Dallas, too," said Randy. "Delphine's not old enough to drive yet, but her parents already bought her this car that's worthy of a queen. Isn't that stupid? Delphine just snaps her fingers and there it is."

"Don't you like Delphine? What goes?"

"Let's just say that some people turn you off and some people turn you on, and leave it at that."

"What about Beth Ann Deering?"

Randy poured milk into a glass and pushed the carton toward me. He forgot to get me a glass. He forgot to get me a plate for my sandwich, too, but I didn't care. I was more interested in his opinion of Beth Ann.

"She hangs around with Delphine," he said. "They're a lot alike. But look, I don't want to influence you pro or con about these girls. Make up your own mind."

"Then I don't suppose I could dig any information out of you about the daughter of Nancy Erskine-Chamberlin."

"How can you even remember a name like that? Sorry, I've never heard of her."

It was a friendly lunch. I liked Randy. He had standards about how far he would go in talking about girls. And it wasn't very far.

I would have to find out about Delphine and Beth Ann myself, and I only had a week. I went home and told my tape recorder. *I have to work fast.* Then I replayed my recording from the night before. It didn't sound all that great. I sounded like I was in shock at my own success.

7

My father complains that he has too much hair on his face and not enough on his head. Every day he has to get rid of the stuff on his face that he yearns to have on his head. But for me, shaving is great. It makes me feel like a man. And I was shaving for Beth Ann Deering.

I was getting ready to go to her house. I had decisions to make. Should I wear my good jacket? It was wrinkled from being in the suitcase. I put it on anyway. After I dressed I looked at myself the way I figured Beth Ann and her parents would look at me. I knew I would pass the test in Phoenix, but was I right for Dallas? Just for one week I wanted to be a Dallas kind of guy.

Jewel and Tony and Mom and Dad had gone out for dinner. Mia had phoned to say that she and Heidi were eating at Delphine's. The maid and Yums and I were alone in the house. I didn't know where in the house the maid was. The maid was her own person. I liked that. She wore a stiff black uniform and a black cap which, in my opinion, belonged on the head nurse in a hospital for the dead. But the maid didn't bother me, because she didn't seem really to be part of bigger-than-life Texas.

I went downstairs and walked toward the back door. This time I wasn't trying to avoid Jewel's crowd of women friends. Beth Ann lived down the street, but she had explained how I could get to her house without walking all the way around front.

I passed the den and I noticed a cowboy hat on the table. It had to be Tony's. It was probably the one he had put on my head at the party.

I went into the den. I put on the hat. I knew it would be too big for me, but I had to see how I looked in it. I already knew how I *felt* in it. Very successful, very Texan.

There was a small mirror in the den. I looked at my reflection. The hat did something for me, something terrific. I wanted to buy one for myself. It probably would cost a fortune. I took off the hat and left the den. For a few moments I had been a new, improved person.

I dashed back to the den, grabbed the hat, and left the house. Tony wouldn't mind. He'd already lent me the hat once without my even asking.

I was surprised how easily I found Beth Ann's house. It was as if the hat on my head guided my way. I was big stuff, that's what I was. I rang the back doorbell. I was just standing there, but I felt like I was walking tall, I was high in the saddle, I was Dallas.

A man dressed in an old shirt and drab pants answered the door and looked up at my hat. Not at me. At my hat. Suddenly I felt as if it were over my face. This man probably knew hats, and he knew mine wasn't mine. I took it off. You're supposed to do that when you go inside anyway. I've seen it in old movies where guys almost always wore hats. Now the only good thing about this hat was that it showed I had enough manners to take it off.

I was still standing outside, but now I was hatless.

A dog came up and started to growl. It was a tiny dog, but it had a big growl. The growl fitted the dog the way the hat fitted me.

"Shut up, Duke!" the man said before he said anything to me.

Duke didn't shut up. He continued growling at me. I was starting to sympathize with Tony and his hatred of the Deerings' dog. I have never kicked a dog in my life, but . . ."

"Hi, Ted." It was Beth Ann, a vision in a crinkly light blue dress that made her dark hair look even darker. I no longer planned to kick her dog.

The man still hadn't spoken to me. I wondered if he was the gardener. Then Beth Ann said, "Dad, this is Ted Fisher." He shook my right hand after I transferred the hat to my left hand.

Beth Ann seemed just as enthusiastic as the night before. She smiled like crazy. We walked inside. It was a big house, like Tony and Jewel's and Randy's, but it looked like an old farmhouse. In the kitchen Beth Ann introduced me to her mother, who was dressed sloppy and was chopping onions over a chop-

43

ping board. Everything looked messy, Mr. and Mrs. Deering dressed badly, and they didn't have a maid. They were my kind of people.

At least I thought so until dinner. They never changed their clothes, but their dining room looked like a palace. We sat at a long, long table that was covered with a thick white tablecloth that had a D in the middle, sewn in gold and circled with gold leaves. Did *D* stand for Dallas or Deering? I didn't ask. And the silverware was gold. The dishes were white with gold leaves. I hadn't seen so much shine since I looked at my body glistening this morning.

Two maids materialized to serve the food. The table was much too big for just Mr. and Mrs. Deering, Beth Ann and me, and all the empty chairs made me nervous. They sat me at the head of the table like I was a visiting king. Beth Ann sat on my right, her parents sat on my left, with her father next to me.

I remembered another long dining table and another Beth Ann. The tables at the ranch where we had stayed just before we came to Dallas and where I had met the other Beth Ann were long like this. But plain. I mean just plain plain. Plain or fancy, long tables had bad vibes.

"So, young man," Mr. Deering said as the first course, slices of fruit in a gold goblet, was being served, "I hear you're from Arizona."

"Yes, and it's a lot like Texas. I mean, it practically *is* Texas."

Beth Ann smiled weakly.

Her father didn't. "Nothing is Texas but Texas."

Mrs. Deering nodded in one hundred percent agreement.

"You're right about that," I added quickly, and I grabbed a gold fork to eat the pieces of fruit at the same time everyone else took a gold spoon. I put down the fork. I had never seen such a collection of spoons, forks and knives at a table. If I was careful and picked up *after* everybody else did, I could be using the same utensil, and not make a fool of myself.

What was I doing here? I should be reading car manuals and exercise books and making wisecracks with Uncle Tony, which I'm often good at, instead of making decisions about forks and spoons. Was it worth it to pass an obstacle course of utensils to get to Beth Ann? Maybe she wasn't even my kind of girl? I don't know what kind of girl is my kind yet, because I'm fifteen and just getting started. For openers, it should probably be a girl who's right at home in a lube pit. I don't even plan to have a gold screwdriver.

Salad came after the fruit cup. I *know* you eat salad with a fork, but I felt nervous about those tiny tomatoes. Do you pierce them with your fork and eat them whole, or cut them up?

"You'll be at your aunt and uncle's for the week?" Mrs. Deering asked.

"Yes."

Mr. Deering pierced his tomato. "Did that uncle of yours ever have a traumatic experience with a dog? He sure hates 'em."

Was I getting in the middle of a fight? I knew whose side I was on. I had a good answer. "No. My uncle *owns* a dog and has for some time. A *quiet* little fellow named Yums."

"That's just a front to hide his canine hatred," said Mr. Deering. He chomped his tomato.

"Yums is a real dog, just like yours, but Tony keeps him inside at night so he won't disturb the neighbors."

I wished Tony could hear me! I wished I had this all down on my tape recorder. I hoped that Beth Ann saw me as a defender of my family's honor and not as a fresh mouth against her father.

"Let's forget dogs and get back to Arizona," she said. Beth Ann cut her tomato with a fork and knife. Now what was I supposed to do with mine?

I wolfed down my tomato whole. I wasn't going to be intimidated. "People keep moving to Arizona," I said. "Our population is growing at a fantastic rate. I live in an extremely popular state."

"It *is* lovely," Mrs. Deering said, as she cut her tomato. "We've visited there a few times. Remember the Grand Canyon, Rock? It was so big you thought it should have been in Texas."

"The Grand Canyon. You can't find a better canyon than that," I added.

Fortunately Beth Ann laughed. That's what she was supposed to do. Then, unfortunately, she made a suggestion, "Tell them about your exciting trip from Phoenix to Dallas."

No way was I going to repeat last night's lies—which I wasn't sure I could remember—or, worse than that, tell them the *truth*. Was Beth Ann an air head? What did she expect me to tell them about?

46

"Tell them about the scenery, Ted, and interesting places to stop along the way."

She was obviously trying to get me to look good to her parents. What a great girl! If I did that, and if I could keep my forks and spoons and knives straight, I might survive the dinner and get Beth Ann. But their table was set for royalty and attended by servants. The Deerings were put on earth to confuse me.

"How is your Tiffany Stew?" Mrs. Deering inquired.

"Tiffany Stew?"

"That's what you're eating. I created it myself."

"Fine. It's great."

I liked the stew, because I knew beyond a doubt that it was supposed to be eaten with a fork. So was the dessert, which was cake with a thick, creamy frosting.

When dinner was over, Mrs. Deering said that we could go and sit in the living room. For more sensational conversation, I guessed. Duke the dog was already there, sitting on a chair. He had been amazingly quiet through dinner. Now I knew why.

Duke was busy chewing away at Tony's hat!

"Bad dog!" Beth Ann yelled as she grabbed the hat away. It was too late. A piece of rim had been chewed off.

"Oh that Duke," said Mrs. Deering. "Just can't keep out of mischief, can you, little dog?"

"Mischief?" I said. "Mischief is chewing an old bedroom slipper. This is—*was*—my uncle's expensive hat!"

"Oh that's no problem," said Mrs. Deering. She left

47

the room and came back with what looked like a checkbook. She sat down, scribbled in it fast, tore something out of the checkbook, and handed it to me.

"Here's a check. This should cover a new hat for your uncle. It it doesn't, let me know."

Mrs. Deering handed me the check.

"One thousand dollars!" I couldn't believe it. "I don't think it costs that much," I managed to say.

"Keep the change," said Mr. Deering.

"I'd prefer the hat the way it was. You don't happen to have one just like it, do you? I don't think I should take this check from you."

"Your uncle wouldn't want *my* hat, believe me," Mr. Deering said.

I believed him.

What was I going to do? Tony would have my head for taking his hat and letting his arch-enemy's dog wreck it. A check from the Deerings could make him more furious.

"Let's not let Duke spoil our perfect evening," Beth Ann said.

Then she touched my arm. "Ted, maybe you should go home right now and face your uncle and get it over with."

"I guess so." I wondered if she wanted to get rid of me? But she seemed so nice, I guess I was feeling paranoid. "Well, thanks everybody for the dinner and thank the maids for serving it and all of that."

"Our pleasure," said Mr. Deering, who seemed friendlier now that I was leaving.

"We enjoyed the evening," Mrs. Deering said. "We like meeting Beth Ann's new friends."

How could she enjoy an evening with a teen-age kid that cost one thousand dollars?

Duke was barking again. "Shut up, Duke!" *I* said it before I could stop myself.

"I'll go out and point the way home," Beth Ann said. "It's dark now."

My expectations of my date with Beth Ann hadn't come close to this evening. I walked out into the night air with a chewed-up hat, a check for one thousand dollars and a smiling Beth Ann Deering.

8

"Over that way," Beth Ann said. She pointed to the right.

We were standing by her swimming pool. I was figuring out how to say goodnight.

"I'm awfully sorry about your uncle's hat," she said. She was making it easier. I figured that meant she really liked me.

"Yeah, I'll have to decide how to break the news to him. Actually, my uncle didn't think it was such a good idea to go to your house. Duke is driving him crazy with his barking all night. Now with this chewed-up hat, Tony will go through the ceiling."

"I thought we'd have such a great evening," Beth Ann said with a sigh—or was it a pout?

"It was great being with you," I reassured her. I wanted her to know I liked her. No act, no exaggeration, just the truth.

"Maybe you'll have a better time when you take Delphine to the movies."

"How did you know about that?"

"I heard her asking you to take her. She did ask you, didn't she?"

Beth Ann sounded like she was competing with Delphine. They were competing for me! Poor girls. I liked that idea.

She kept talking. "Delphine thinks she's sophisticated for her age. Some of the other girls watch her and copy her."

"Oh," was all I could think of to say. This was interesting information. I wondered if I'd have to *choose* between the girls. Did the rivalry just start the night before and over me? I wondered but I didn't want to think about it. I was supposed to call Delphine and take her to the movies. I hardly knew either of them, but Beth Ann standing in the moonlight in her blue dress and talking in her soft drawl seemed about as terrific as any girl could be. But if Delphine was really sophisticated—well anything could happen.

"You have good teeth," Beth Ann said. "They shine in the moonlight."

Suddenly she kind of leaned over and up, kissed me on the cheek and ran back into her house. The kiss felt like a flower petal or something brushing my face.

I stood there by her pool, with the big chewed-up hat and the check in my hand. I was hypnotized. I had just been given a gentle kiss and a compliment that belonged to a vampire, and I loved it.

But I had to go home and face Tony.

I almost lost my way in the dark. But I had a sense of direction, because I could hear Duke barking, and that told me where I had come from. I hurried the other way. What a blasted, noisy dog!

The back door of the house was unlocked. I went inside. I heard voices in the living room. I looked down at the chewed-up hat. This was it.

Mom, Dad, Mia and Heidi were sitting around the living room. No Tony, no Jewel. For a minute it seemed as if we were back on the road, just the five of us in a motel. I thought of all the problems we had already faced together on this vacation trip—the noisy motel guests, the roaches, the missed exits, the people we wished we hadn't met, all the stuff that had annoyed us and united us at the same time. But this hat catastrophe was mine alone.

Mia looked up. "Hi, Ted. How did it go?"

"It was wonderful."

"Why don't I believe you?" Mia said, in her big sister voice.

"Because I'm lying," I said. I sat down beside her on the sofa. "Where's Jewel and Tony?"

"They went out to buy ten gallons of ice cream," said Mom, smiling.

"Is that a joke? Am I supposed to laugh about ten gallons?" I fingered the hat. It was a ten-gallon hat, that's what it was called. Duke must have reduced it to seven gallons.

Did I imagine that my family was staring at the hat, which was now on my lap?

"Where did you get that hat?" Heidi asked. "Did you go shopping today?"

"No, I went borrowing."

"It's Tony's?" my father asked. "Good of him to lend it to you. Although I guess it's one of his old ones. Kind of beat-up-looking, isn't it?"

"He didn't lend it to me."

Maybe my family would back me up. We had united for an "us against the world" attitude on this trip. Of course, now the world was Tony and Jewel. And they were family too.

I had to explain. "You'll never believe this, but while you were all busy having dinner, something happened. On the way out to Beth Ann's I saw this hat just sitting by itself in the den and I thought it would be fun to wear it. So, I put it on and went over to Beth Ann's. Then I took it off because that's the polite thing to do, you know. But while I was eating dinner Duke, their dog, was eating dinner, too. *This!*" I held up the hat so that everyone could get a good look at the chewed-up rim. "This hat was in perfect shape when I put it on."

"Oh no!" Mia groaned. "Uncle Tony loathes that dog and I bet he loves that hat."

Heidi giggled. "Boy, we haven't had any trouble since we hit Dallas. I was missing trouble but now it's back. Good old Ted."

I held up the check. "There's a ray of hope—I mean, that Tony won't kill me. Mrs. Deering gave me a check for damages made out to Tony for one thousand dollars."

"Oh wow," said Heidi. "Tony can buy ten hats for that. I've got an old swimsuit, Ted. Take it over to the Deerings' dog and bring me back a check. I'm not going to be a pig about this. I'll take three hundred dollars."

My father was frowning. "Tony won't accept their check. He's so angry at the Deerings he'll tear it up in frustration."

"I thought of that," I said.

"You'll just have to tell Tony as soon as he and Jewel come back," my mother said. "Oh Ted, I was hoping everything would run smoothly here."

"Why should it?" said Heidi. "Isn't trouble part of every vacation?"

"Heidi, come on," said Mia. "Listen, I wished I had one thousand dollars today. I could have spent it in just one store. Delphine and her mother took us to these fabulous shops."

"Yeah, it was their idea of sightseeing in Dallas," said Heidi. "I wanted to look at swimming pools shaped like kidneys and hearts and stuff."

"What do you think of Delphine?" I asked Mia. I was fishing.

"You mean what does she think of you," she answered. "I know how your mind works, Ted."

"Same as yours, Mia."

"I'm not interested in what any guy thinks of me any more. Except Neal. And I *know* how he feels. He didn't call today, did he? He's going to call me here. He promised."

I shrugged. "I don't know. I was over at Randy's part of the day, and I was out tonight."

Mia sighed. "I guess not. You're the last person I've asked. Maybe I'll stick around the house tomorrow, so I won't miss his call."

54

"What if he doesn't call tomorrow? You could spend your entire time in Dallas waiting for that call." Mom seemed annoyed.

"There's plenty to do here, Mother. And some things are worth waiting for," said Mia. "I'm in love. It's no secret."

I was glad not to be talking about the hat anymore. But I wished Mia had given me a straight answer about Delphine. "So what are the plans tomorrow for the people who aren't in love with Neal Guest?" I asked.

"Tony and Jewel haven't told us yet," said Dad, and he groaned. Then he added, "But you can bet they will."

Mom smiled at Dad. "I'm going to have a little talk with Jewel about her overplanning our stay in Dallas. That party, almost the minute we arrived. This morning's brunch. Who knows what tomorrow. I couldn't say anything about the party and the brunch, because they were already arranged."

"You should have known, Mom," said Mia. "You know Jewel."

"She wasn't this bad in Pittsburgh," said Dad. "Maybe there isn't as much to plan for in Pittsburgh."

I joined in. "She treats us like she's our mother."

"You don't really mind, do you?" asked Mom. "It means so much to her. She doesn't have children all year long. And it's only temporary."

Heidi answered for me. "See, Ted, on the road, no matter what the hassles, it was *our* vacation. Here I think we're Tony and Jewel's property."

Heidi seemed satisfied with herself for figuring this

out. But she didn't stop. "Listen, Ted, you'll be lucky if Jewel and Tony are still speaking to you after they see Tony's hat."

"Not funny," I said. We were back to the hat, and we all sat around not saying anything more until the door opened and Jewel and Tony and Yums walked in.

9

Jewel and Tony were loaded down with cartons of ice cream.

"Real food!" said Heidi. She wasn't kidding.

"Ten different flavors," Jewel said, grinning. "I thought it would be fun to have an ice-cream party for just the family before we went to bed."

An ice-cream party? Jewel had parties on the brain. I didn't remember her as party crazy when she lived in Pittsburgh.

I stood up and walked over to Tony. I held up the hat. I said, "Before we have any party, I've got something to tell you. This is, *was*, your hat. I saw it in the den and, well, I wore it over to the Deerings and, well, their dog did *this!*"

Tony stared at the hat. Then he said, "My four-hundred-dollar hat. That yapping mongrel chewed up my four-hundred-dollar hat."

Heidi gave a little scream. "Four hundred dollars! You're in luck, Ted."

"What does that mean?" Tony asked.

"That means, how would you like to clear a profit of six hundred dollars, Uncle Tony," Mia answered. *Uncle* Tony sounded real familylike.

"I still don't get it." He wasn't smiling.

I gave the check to Tony. "Mrs. Deering wrote you a check for one thousand dollars for the damage to your hat. See, it even says on it, after the word *For:* Duke damage hat."

Tony fingered and gazed at the check. "Very interesting," he said. I couldn't tell if he seemed happy with it or unhappy. He was analyzing it.

"Is it interesting good or bad?" I asked.

"Because they admit that their dog is guilty of property damage it's interesting good. If I can't stop his yelping at night, I might be able to get at him from this angle. I need a lawyer."

Dad spoke up. "Can't you just talk to Rock Deering, Tony?"

"No Dad. You don't talk to this guy," I said, answering for Tony. "I had dinner with the Deerings, and Mr. Deering isn't great on conversation. You have to like Texas and you have to like his dog just to get a polite word out of him. Actually it's strange—they live like rich peasants or poor royalty. Except that Beth Ann seems normal."

Tony put his hand on my shoulder. "Perceptive kid. You did a good job tonight."

Heidi just about exploded in laughter.

I was feeling relieved until Mom spoke up. "Tony,

ed shouldn't have taken your hat without your permission. He really didn't do a good job, as you put it."

"Okay, so he lucked out," said Tony, waving the check. "He got me a guilty check from the Deering weirdos."

"He sure did," said Jewel, and she squeezed Tony like they were having a big celebration. I was getting more of a feeling about how they had changed since they moved to Dallas. Now they had a certain style of life—lots of parties, no kids, lots of money. They weren't used to disciplining or depriving anymore.

Tony put on the hat and strode around the room like a happy giant. "Time for a celebration," Jewel said. Then she dished out the ice cream. Heidi had the most, of course. This time it felt like a party to me. Until Jewel turned to me. "Almost forgot to tell you, Ted. I've arranged for you to go out with Nancy Erskine-Chamberlin's daughter, Laura."

"But—" I looked at Mom. She kind of shrugged and gave me her be-a-good-boy smile.

"I've already arranged it," said Jewel. "You don't want to disappoint the poor girl, do you?"

Heidi nodded yes, but I was the only one who saw her.

Jewel put her arm around me and asked if I wanted more pistachio or chocolate.

"Vanilla," I answered. I had to show *some* independence.

When I got to my room, it was hard to explain my evening to my tape recorder. But I tried. I used almost one entire side of tape.

10

The telephone rang the next morning during break fast. Mia rushed to answer it. "It's Neal. I know it's Neal."

The maid reached the phone first. She answered it then turned and said, "It's for me."

The maid actually had a telephone call. Someone must know her, know her name, know she exists. She said, "Yes, yes," and hung up.

Mia sat down at the table again.

"Neal will call," I said. I liked the guy. He'd been nice on the road. I wanted him to call. I was feeling successful about love, and I wanted Mia to feel the same way. Last night Beth Ann had acted as if she really liked me. A compliment about teeth is unusual. A girl has to think about that kind of compliment before she makes it. It's easy and slick to say something good about a guy's smile. But teeth, that's deep

I had to plan what I would do next about Beth Ann. Of course I had to keep Delphine in mind too.

The telephone rang again. Mia beat the maid out this time. Could the maid possibly have *two* friends? But the first call was probably from the laundry telling her that her hospital-for-the-dead uniform was starched and pressed and ready to be picked up.

Mia said, "Hello, Neal." How could she be so confident? How could she be so dumb? It wasn't Neal. She turned to me. "It's for you, Ted."

Mia handed me the receiver. Before I could say hello, I heard a girl's voice on the end of the line. "Hello there."

I answered back, "Hello there." I didn't know who was calling me, but I had to say something.

"Guess who."

Was it Beth Ann? Was it Delphine? Their Texas voices sounded alike to me.

She continued. "Don't you know me? Theodore, it's *Delphine*."

"Sure, Delphine. You didn't give me a chance. And what's this Theodore business?"

"That's your real name, isn't it? Ted is short for Theodore. It's a nice name, Theodore Fisher."

"My name's Ted."

"Your legal name's Ted?"

"That's it."

"I like the name Ted."

"Thanks."

Long pause.

"Ted, have you seen any good movies lately?"

I think it was a hint.

Delphine didn't wait for me to answer. "How about seeing one with me tonight, Ted?"

"Sounds great."

"I'll pick you up around seven. Okay?"

"You'll pick *me* up?"

"Of course," said Delphine. "Unless you can get your uncle's car?"

"No. No. You come get me."

"Can't wait," said Delphine.

"Neither can I. What movie are we seeing?"

"I'll pick out something good."

"That's good." It wasn't easy talking to Delphine on the telephone. I felt like I was reacting instead of taking charge. Still, I couldn't believe my luck. Two dates in a row. Two beautiful girls. This never happened in Phoenix.

Three dates. When I got off the telephone, Jewel said, "You didn't make a date for tonight, did you Ted? You're supposed to be going out with Laura Erskine-Chamberlin."

"You didn't tell me it was for tonight."

"Well how many nights do you have in Dallas? If you want to have a meaningful relationship here, you don't have much time."

"A meaningful relationship?" Dad roared. "Ted's a long way from that, Jewel. He's only fifteen."

"I want to think that I at least contributed to a proper social life while he was in Dallas."

I had more contributions than I could handle.

"Jewel," I said, "it's great of you to think of me, but I already know two girls, and they're both after me. I mean, *after* me."

62

Mia looked at me in a puzzled way.

Jewel sighed. "Very well, I'll give you Laura's phone number and you two work out another night to meet."

"I have to call a strange girl?"

Heidi giggled. "Those are the kind you like, Ted."

After breakfast, Tony and Dad left for golf or riding or something. I wondered how Dad felt about Tony having all this land and the house and everything that was so much bigger than what we had back home. Did it make a difference that Tony was his brother-in-law and not his brother? Jewel and Mom loved each other, and Dad seemed to like Tony. But deep down did he resent the Texas Tony? The Pittsburgh Tony hadn't been any problem.

Mom had a job to do. At breakfast Jewel had announced the "itinerary" for the day, and Mom had said, "Jewel, where is it written that we must have an itinerary? After breakfast I'm going to stretch out by the pool. I want you to stretch out by the pool. And we'll talk like old-fashioned sisters from the old home town."

Mom and Jewel were now stretched out on lounges by the pool. I was sure that Mom was doing most of the talking.

Heidi, Mia and I were left alone at the table. Heidi got up. "I'm going over to Beth Ann's and try out her pool. She invited me the other night."

"Don't forget to take a spare swimsuit for Duke to rip," I said.

"Do you think it would work? Would it look suspicious if I stuck it in his mouth? I could use any

63

amount of money."

Mia laughed. "Oh, Heidi, just have a good time."

"I will."

Heidi ran to get one or two swimsuits.

Mia turned to me. "Alone at last," she said.

"What do you mean?"

"I mean let's have a brother-sister chat."

"Everybody's having talks around here this morning. Must be contagious. But why us? Need some advice about Neal?"

"No! He'll call."

"Anything else I can help you with?"

Mia sipped the remains of her orange juice. The maid hadn't taken away the breakfast dishes yet. She must be hiding again.

Mia put down her glass. "Ted, you can't help me, but I can help you. You are presently in over your head."

"Over my head?"

"Way over."

"How?"

"Look, Ted. You're a great brother, and if I were a girl—I mean, if I weren't your sister I'd be happy to be your girlfriend. Maybe I'm not putting this right. I mean you're the kind of guy that a sincere, intelligent girl would really go for and appreciate. But some girls don't know how to appreciate the qualities you have."

"Aha! Light is dawning. You're talking about Beth Ann and Delphine. Or one of them."

"Both of them."

"Now, wait a minute. Forty-eight hours ago you hadn't even met these girls, and now you know all about them? You're the one who glanced at a guy in a rest-stop restaurant and decided he was worth meeting. He turned out to be worth meeting, but you just jumped in."

"Ted, what I'm saying is that I recognize these girls. I recognize their type. They're—uh—it's not a nice word, but I think they're *users*. You're the new guy in town, and they each want to score points by getting you. You're something to acquire. Like a horse."

"A *horse*? I'm getting mad, Mia."

"No, I didn't mean it that way. Right now you're the newest thing around. These girls have got big houses, horses, pools, the works. They're competing for the best of everything."

"Now you're talking. You went off track with that horse business. If they want to think *I'm* the best of everything, let them."

"But it's a *game*. They're not sincere. Remember that girl we met at the ranch. Her name was Beth Ann too. That's the type. It's not your fault, it's theirs. They're bad news."

"You're telling me my good news is bad news."

"I'm sorry. I know you don't want to hear it."

"You think you know everything just because you've finally got a decent boyfriend?"

"I've got a boyfriend who appreciates me. Remember that guy Kip we met at a motel? He *seemed* to like me. But I caught on to him quick."

"You're smarter than I am, right?"

"Older. And I'm a girl. I know *girls*."

"You're wrong. Beth Ann and Delphine—well, I think I'm their dream guy or something."

"I hope you are. But I don't think you are. Just watch out, okay?"

"Mia, you're getting to be too old for your age. Be my sister and not my mother or aunt pretending to be my sister."

"What does that mean?"

"Guess." Suddenly I was mad at the great state of Texas for confusing me.

Mom and Jewel were coming down the stairs. Jewel was saying, "Now, Gwen, if you don't want to go to lunch, we'll stay in. I'll cancel the appointment with the girls."

"What girls?"

"A few of my friends. There's this new restaurant I thought you'd like—"

Jewel stopped talking when she saw me. She pulled a piece of paper out of her shirt pocket and handed it to me. "Here's Laura's number. Do be nice to her when you call her. She's really a lovely girl."

"Mothers' daughters aren't lovely."

"That doesn't make any sense."

"It does when you're fifteen. Okay, I'll call her right now and get it over with."

Jewel looked disturbed and turned back to my mother.

I went to my room to make the phone call. I

considered this call the nothing highlight of my vacation in Dallas.

I dialed Laura's number.

A man answered.

"May I speak to Laura, please?"

"One minute."

It was a short minute. Laura must have been right there. I could imagine her having tried to beat the man to the telephone. Girls whose mothers make dates for them are hard up for phone calls.

"Hello." She sounded like Beth Ann and Delphine. Girls in Texas all sound alike.

"Laura?"

"Yes."

"My name is Ted Fisher. Maybe your mother told you about me. I'm visiting my aunt and uncle, Jewel and Tony Mayne. I'm from Arizona."

"Yes, Mom mentioned you. Welcome to Texas."

"Thanks, but I'm not staying here very long. I'm hardly staying here at all. And that's why I have to break the date that my aunt arranged with your mother for us for tonight."

"I'm sorry. You sound like an interesting person to know."

"I do?"

I felt awful. She had a nice way of saying I'm sorry, and she had insight. Interesting person. I couldn't wait to tell my tape I was a hit yet again.

"Maybe we could make it for another night." The words came out of me before I even knew what I was saying. Who was this girl anyway?

"What night?"

She wasn't supposed to say *what night*. She was supposed to say *maybe*. This girl didn't play games.

"Aren't you busy? It's your summer vacation."

"I'm not busy this week."

Bad sign. Nobody wanted to be busy with her.

"Tomorrow night?" She was asking.

Everyone wanted to go out with me. Maybe this Laura was falling for me right over the telephone. I hadn't even tried to make an impression on her. Except maybe a bad one, for breaking a date.

I answered, "I'm not sure about tomorrow night. I've got this situation where—"

I couldn't tell Laura Erskine-Chamberlin about Beth Ann and Delphine.

I went on. "I have a friend who's dating two girls at kind of the same time and I'm helping him out with this particular situation. I might be tied up tomorrow night helping him out."

"I don't understand."

"It's simple. Both girls are after him, and he's dating both, and I'm acting as his adviser."

"Why does he need advice?"

"It's confusing being pursued by two girls."

"Your friend sounds like the kind of guy I wouldn't want to be with. Superman or something. He's just too perfect. I hope you're not like that. You sound like a nice guy, giving him advice. Does he like one girl better than the other?"

"He doesn't know either one of them very well."

"So you just tell your friend that he should keep his

head on straight until he gets to know these girls."

"You sound very positive. Do you always sound so positive?"

"When I know what I'm talking about, I do."

"I'll tell him what you said. I'll call you back and let you know how everything turns out, and then maybe we can go out."

"Okay. Goodbye."

She was off the phone. She was kind of no-nonsense direct. I bet she never giggled in her life. I didn't want to go out with her. No way.

I needed to think. I needed to confide in my tape recorder. *This girl, Laura, doesn't want a Superman. She doesn't want anybody too perfect. She said I sound like a nice guy. Maybe she'd understand that I'm just a guy from Phoenix and not a Texas millionaire. Would she? Would she appreciate the real me? If I could only remember who the real me is.*

12

Delphine and her mother picked me up for the date. I had never been out on a date with a girl *and* her mother. They drove up in a fabulous car, long, sleek. I loved it. But Delphine seemed to *need* the car, like it was surgically attached to her. I could tell the way she sat in it that the car meant everything to her.

Delphine's mother, a beautiful blond, looked so much like Delphine that I knew just what Delphine was going to look like in twenty or thirty years. Not bad. But I hoped her mother wouldn't go into the movies with us.

She didn't. We didn't go to a movie. Delphine explained, "I couldn't find any movie that looked interesting, so I decided that we should go out to dinner."

"Dinner?" I reached into my pocket. Tony had stuffed a twenty-dollar bill into it just as I left the house. I had protested. Mom had protested. Dad had protested. Jewel had cheered him on. I had planned to give it back tomorrow. Now I didn't know if I'd have it to give back. What if dinner cost a hundred dollars? This was Dallas.

"I tried to make reservations for the theater," Delphine said. "But they were all sold out. No wonder. The actors hang from the ceiling and sit in umbrellas and they wallpaper bathtubs on stage and say very profound things while they're doing it. But you've probably seen even more sophisticated stuff."

"Yeah, oh sure." What was she *talking* about? It sounded gross.

The car, with Delphine's mother at the wheel, glided along. Delphine was sitting in back beside me. It was unreal. My luck was too much— money, two blonds, a fantastic car. Last night a dinner with gold silverware and a different attractive girl. How did I get to deserve all of this?

Easy. By lying. Face it, telling a bunch of tall tales gave me this reward. What if Beth Ann and Delphine knew the truth? What if? Maybe they'd dump me. Why did I have to get an attack of conscience when I was getting a ride in the car of my dreams!

I started to think about what Mia had said. That I was just something for Delphine and Beth Ann to compete for. Mia was so off base. I was getting this fancy treatment because Delphine and Beth Ann were both crazy about me. Maybe I could kind of ease into the truth with the girls, tell them I exaggerated just a little about my trip. Drop a few hints. I needed for them to like the *real* Ted Fisher.

The restaurant was a salad bar in a shopping center. I was surprised. But it was better than walking into a ritzy restaurant where I might feel out of place. There was a shoe store, a dry-cleaning place, a bakery, a flower shop, and a few other businesses in the center.

"Surprised?" Delphine's mother asked as she pulled up to the salad bar. "This place has fabulous carrots. Phone me when you want to get picked up."

At least she wasn't going to hang around with us all night. I thanked her for the ride, and Delphine and I got out of the car. The minute we were outside Delphine took my hand and asked, "How did it go at Beth Ann's last night?"

"How did you know I was at Beth Ann's?"

"I knew."

"Beth Ann knew that you asked me to go to the movies with you. You two compare notes or something?"

"What ever do you mean by that?"

"Are you two friends?"

"We're fast, firm friends. What do you think of her? Have you seen the family car? It's a pick-up truck. Show-offs!"

Delphine kept clutching my hand. "Lots of my friends come to this salad bar. I want them to meet you."

She was proud of me. I wondered if she was proud of her horse, too. Why did Mia have to say that to me!

"The broccoli's great here." Delphine was looking into the window of Salad Daze.

"I don't eat broccoli. It's against my religion."

"They put melted cheese on it, and croutons and stuff. C'mon."

Delphine walked ahead of me into the house of broccoli. She waved to some kids at a table. "C'mon," she said to me again. We walked up to the table. A bunch of girls were sitting there. Delphine said, "I want you to meet a very special friend of mine, Theodore Fisher. He's come all the way from Arizona."

The girls really stared at me. It was not the worst feeling in the world, but something else was—the way Delphine had introduced me. It sounded as if I had come all the way from Arizona to see her. She also knew my name wasn't Theodore. Wasn't just plain Ted good enough for her?

We went on to the next table, where some guys and girls were sitting. Delphine repeated her introduction. Then she steered me to the salad bar. Everything that could possibly be done to a vegetable had been done to the vegetables there. Actually it was a nice spread, and the food looked tempting. I didn't recognize the broccoli until after I put some on my plate.

We filled up our plates, and went to join some of her friends. "By the way," she said, "if anyone asks, you're a freshman in college. Okay?"

It wasn't okay. How could I tell her that? Easy. I would admit to Delphine that I was only fifteen years old. I whispered to her, "I'm fifteen years old."

She smiled and patted my hand. Didn't she hear me? Didn't she care? Lying about my age had been

74

one of my major lies. This was really weird. Well, if she didn't hear me, at least I had tried. I had told the absolute truth. Did she like me for myself no matter what my age? Suddenly I thought of Laura. She popped into my head. Laura? How could I think of a person I didn't even want to have a blind date with at a time like this? Just because Laura was honest over the phone and Delphine seemed—I didn't want to think about it. For the first time since I met Delphine, I felt real. But I couldn't enjoy the feeling, because I kept wondering if she was.

I dug into my unreal broccoli.

Mom and Jewel were having a fight when I got home from my date with Delphine. Mom was saying, "I did not give Heidi permission to go swimming in Beth Ann's pool. I did not give Heidi permission to leave the house. She's not familiar with this neighborhood."

"But Gwen, it's just a hop and a skip to Beth Ann's house. Heidi couldn't get lost. The Deerings' dog is like a beacon the way he barks."

"So you gave her permission."

"Well, yes. You were getting dressed and Heidi said Beth Ann invited her, and I said fine. You've let me give the kids permission before. Now you've changed your mind. You know what? You're treating me like a kid. First you say it's okay if I do something and then you say it's not. We need some rules around here. We even need some rules to say who's going to make the rules."

I saw Jewel put a finger to the corner of her eye. She was trying to keep from crying. "I hardly ever see any of you, and I'm really trying to make everyone's vacation perfect. I know Dallas, I know people, and I don't want you to miss anything. Heidi had a wonderful time at Beth Ann's. Admit it. And why are you getting mad now? You had all day to get mad. I told you this morning."

"That was before I found out that their dog bit her swimsuit. She could have been in it."

"No, she couldn't have, Mom."

Mom and Jewel hardly paid attention to what I had just said. Kids who enter adult fights don't get much respect.

Mom said wearily, "You home? Have a good time?"

"It was okay. But listen, Heidi took an extra swimsuit over to the Deerings'. At least she said she might. She wanted Duke to take a thousand-dollar bite out of it. She probably stuck it in his mouth."

"Oh no!" Jewel threw up her arms. She started to scream with laughter. Mom joined her. Then Mom put her hand on Jewel's arm. "Oh Jewel, excuse me for flying off the handle. I'm just kind of knocked out. Honestly I don't think I've recuperated from our long drive here."

"Look, what's a sister for if we can't have a few fights. It's hard to have them with strangers. Sometimes they never forgive you."

"Sometimes you don't want them to." Now Mom squeezed Jewel's arm, and they both went into another fit of laughter. I knew Mom was tired. I could tell. I hoped that after the visit was over they

77

wouldn't remember the fight and feel bad. It wasn't as if they lived next door to each other and had lots of chances to share good times.

"I'm going to bed," I said.

"A truly brilliant idea," said Jewel. "Tomorrow will be a lovely day, I just know it."

I bent down and kissed Mom and Jewel good night. I usually don't kiss Mom good night, but this gave me an excuse to kiss Jewel, and I thought she needed as much support as possible. This still didn't mean I was going out with Nancy Erskine-Chamberlin's daughter.

I went upstairs to my room. I tried to talk to my tape recorder, but I wasn't ready. I had a lot to think about first. Delphine had wanted me to say I was a college freshman. She knew that was a lie. She also knew I had lied to her about my age. If she had a brain in her head—and I think she did—she probably knew that all my exaggerations had been lies. By accepting them, *she* was lying. I picked up my tape recorder. I pressed a button. *"I admitted to Delphine that I'm only fifteen. She knows I lied to her. She ignored it. Why is she interested in me? Why is Beth Ann interested in me? Does Beth Ann know the truth too?"* Questions, questions. Mia had an answer I didn't want to think about. Fortunately my tape ran out. I put a fresh tape in the recorder. Tomorrow my head might be more clear. I went to bed.

"Woof! Woof, woof, woof!"

A dog was barking. A dog was howling. It was Duke. I had never heard him from my bedroom. Now he sounded as if he were outside my window. I went to the window. I couldn't see anything.

He kept on barking. No wonder Tony was furious. Tony and Jewel's bedroom was closer to the Deering house than mine. I felt like I was back in that noisy motel where we had to change rooms in the middle of the night. I went back to the window, which was closed because we had air conditioning. I opened it. I yelled "Shut up you beast!" and I slammed it shut.

I knew the beast couldn't hear me, but everything finally got quiet anyway. I went back to bed and pulled my covers around me. I willed myself to dream that Duke had taken a big bite out of Delphine's car. But it didn't work. I dreamed about Arizona.

14

I went over to Randy's house before breakfast. He was swimming in his pool. "I came to pick your brain," I said. "It's older and more experienced than mine."

Randy laughed as he climbed out of the pool and dried himself off with a towel. "What makes you think I have a brain to pick?"

"I know that you know Beth Ann Deering and Delphine Rasmussen well enough *not* to talk about them. Is there something to hide?"

Randy sat down at the edge of the pool. "That's not the point, Ted. I've drawn my conclusions, I have my opinions, but they don't have to be your conclusions or opinions. You're entitled to your own."

"But you've been around them. You live on their block. You've seen them in action. Didn't all of you grow up together?"

"I'm much older than they are. I'm a senior in college. They're high-school kids like you."

"Are they best friends?"

"Let's just say they're going to make great executives some day. They each have a strong competitive streak. Competitors can be friends, but there's always that little edge, that one-up kind of thing."

I sat down beside Randy. "I'm not bragging now, really. They're both making a big play for me. Should I be suspicious? My sister Mia says I should watch out."

Randy shrugged. "Just because they're competitive doesn't mean they don't like you."

I wanted to tell Randy more. I wanted to tell him about the college-freshman business. But I was so happy with his answer that I didn't want to spoil it.

"Change of subject," I said. "Do you date anybody special?"

"Nope."

"Would you like to?"

"Depends."

"I'm supposed to go out with that Nancy Erskine-Chamberlin's daughter. She might be a little young for you, but—"

Randy raised his hand. "Oh no you don't. Blind dates—forget it."

"Maybe she's nice. She sounds nice."

"Let me know."

"I can't do that, because I'm not going out with her."

"How are you going to get out of it?"

"Any suggestions?"

"Yeah. Borrow one of my swim trunks, jump in the pool with me and wash all those girls right out of your hair."

"But I'm supposed to call her."

"Then call her. It's simple."

Randy's idea of simple was not mine. But I decided to call Laura as soon as I got back to the house. I had to get it over with. I would tell her I was too busy to go out with her.

Back at the house, everyone was sitting around the living room looking tired.

"That blasted dog!" Dad said.

"You too?" I asked.

Jewel nodded. "Everybody. We all heard Duke."

"I'm going over and tell off the Deerings!" This last remark came from Mom. Mom had a special talent for telling people off when her cause was noble and right.

"How about all of us going over? Just like with Bruce Valentine, the night clerk at the motel before we came here?" This came from Heidi.

"I'll even risk missing Neal's phone call," Mia added.

"*I* want to do it," I said. "By myself. I know the Deerings. And, besides, I want to see Beth Ann again."

I was sorry I said that. But it was true. Mia gave me a peculiar look. But she said, "Let Ted go alone. He knows what he's doing."

Heidi spoke up. "You tell them off, Ted. Their dog bit my swimsuit yesterday and all they did was offer to buy me a new suit. No money or anything. They've gotten cheap."

82

"I'll eat, make one very quick phone call, and I'm off," I said.

"Fine," said Jewel.

Everyone was smiling. We were all in harmony. This was the first time since we arrived in Dallas that everyone had agreed on an activity. Now we were one big family, because Tony and Jewel were included in it. If we only lived near each other we wouldn't have to worry about how to spend a short time together. We would have a nice, spread-out, long time together.

"Don't let them ruffle you, son," Tony said. "If you have any problems, I'll go straight to my attorney with their Duke damage check."

Did anyone notice that Tony called me son? I guess it's just an expression. I still had his twenty dollars. I forgot to give it back. I'd have to get it out of the pocket of the pants I wore last night. But first things first. We all ate breakfast.

After breakfast I went up to my room and called Laura. I had her number right on my dresser. With any luck, I'd be throwing it away in three minutes.

Laura answered the phone.

"Hi," I said. "This is Ted Fisher calling with a bit of bad news."

"Tell me fast. That's the best way to unload bad news."

"It isn't that kind of bad news."

"Then it must be about your friend and his romantic problems. The friend you're advising."

"It seems to be a continuing situation. That's why I won't—"

"What happened?"

So much for my three minute conversation. All I wanted to do was tell Laura I wouldn't be able to take her out period. But she wanted details. She sounded concerned.

"Not important. But—"

"Listen, it may not be important to you, but I'll bet it's important to your friend, and since you've already confided in me I want to know if he's all right. Did he find out something about the girl he took out last night?"

"Yes, he did. You're very perceptive."

"What did he find out?"

"I can't tell you. See, I was calling because it's possible that I have a head cold."

"I'm sorry."

When she gave me her sincere "I'm sorry" it made me feel like a rat.

"It's just a possibility."

"Well, you should stay in and nurse it. But what will your friend do if you're sick and can't give him advice?"

"He'll just have to manage on his own."

"You should tell him to stay cool and to be proud of himself, because if a person isn't proud of himself he won't respect his own opinions. Actually, it sounds to me like your friend doesn't respect his own opinions."

"You think so? You may have something there. Go on."

What was happening? I didn't want to hang up.

"Go on? There isn't anything else to say. Not right now. And what I just said, that's just common sense, right?"

"Yeah, I guess. Thanks, Laura. Laura, were you named after that old movie *Laura*? I know a few Lauras who were." I was trying to be friendly. She deserved it.

"You've got it. My folks say I look like Gene Tierney who played Laura. Do you look like Dana Andrews? He fell for her. It would be fun to meet someone who looked like him."

"No, I don't look anything like he looked in that movie. And about meeting you—"

Here was my chance. Goodbye, so long.

"I'll call you back about that, Laura. Okay?"

"Okay. Identify yourself as Dana. Just because it's more fun that way."

"All right."

"Goodbye, Dana." She hung up.

I wondered if *Laura* was playing on TV. Gene Tierney was a fox in it, if I remember right. I took my tape recorder out of my pocket and spoke into it. I surprised myself. The recorder was supposed to help me with Delphine and Beth Ann. It wasn't for Laura. But I asked the recorder: *"Am I getting interested in Laura? No! Life is already too complicated. Dana Andrews signing off."*

15

On the way to Beth Ann's house, I thought about what Laura had said. I was proud of myself for what I was doing right now, but I wasn't proud of the way I had acted with Delphine and Beth Ann. Did I really need to make up stories and exaggerate so much? Did I really need to pretend I was a lady-killer? Laura would say no.

Not that I *needed* Laura's advice. Just the night before, I had admitted to Delphine that I was only fifteen. I did that on my own. How would Beth Ann take the truth? First I had to take care of the dog problem. Maybe she wouldn't be speaking to me after that, anyway. But I owed this to Tony and Jewel.

As I rang the doorbell I thought about the compliment Beth Ann had given me on my teeth. It gave me confidence.

Teeth! I saw Duke's as Beth Ann opened the door. But he wasn't biting, he was only barking.

"What a nice surprise!" Beth Ann exclaimed when she saw me.

It wasn't going to be a nice surprise.

"Come in," Beth Ann said. "How was your date last night?"

She asked, just like that. She was really keeping track.

"Okay."

"Is that all? Sounds boring."

She looked hopeful. Did she really want me to have a bad time with her friend? What kind of friends were they?

"Tell me about it. Where did she take you?"

"Take me?"

"In her car, silly."

"You knew we went out in her car?"

"Delphine and her car are what you would call inseparable. Except she doesn't have a driver's license, so her mother took you, right?"

Beth Ann led me into the kitchen while she questioned me. I sat down in a chair. No one was around. It would have been better to have the whole family present.

"Beth Ann, I came to talk about your dog. He kept all of us up last night. He barked and barked and barked."

"I slept like a log."

"Uncle Tony said that owners are never kept up by their own dogs. It's the neighbors who suffer."

"You're suffering?"

"It's not funny. Are your parents home? I'd like to talk to them."

"Duke's my dog, too."

"Then you've got to keep him shut up at night."

"You want me to tell him to shut up?"

"I said this wasn't funny. Keep him indoors. Or my Uncle Tony will take legal steps."

"The police?"

The police sounded like a good idea to me. The police are free, and lawyers cost money. Money probably didn't mean much to Tony, but what the heck. "Yeah, the police."

"You're tough," she said. She fluttered her eyelashes.

"No I'm not."

"You're a real man. For fifteen years old, you're a real man."

"How did *you* know my age?"

I already knew how she knew. She also knew about the date with Delphine. The details. The mother with the car. She didn't guess. She was told. By Delphine. The only thing she didn't know was if I had a good time.

Beth Ann had a question to answer. "You told me," she said. "You told me you were fifteen."

"No, I didn't."

"Oh well. Fifteen, twenty-five, eighty—what difference does it make?"

"It makes a difference. Truth and lies make a difference."

"Weren't we talking about Duke?"

"Okay. Back to Duke. Inside or outside?"

"I'll check with my folks. I'll tell them that your uncle might call the police."

"Tonight he'll call the police if your dog yaps. In Arizona we have laws against noise."

"Tell me all about Arizona."

"Why do you keep changing subjects?"

"Do I?"

"Yes."

"When are we going out together?"

"There you go."

"I want to see you again, Ted, and not to talk about dogs. I want you to meet my friends."

"Do they hang out in salad bars?"

"No, those are Delphine's friends. A lot of her friends are the same as mine, and a lot are different."

"Sounds like you're loaded with friends."

"I'm popular. Can't help it. So how about tonight? There's a party a few streets away. We can walk. No mother, no automobile. Say yes."

She was beautiful, she was begging me, and nothing else seemed to be important. What Mia had told me fizzled, what Laura advised me fizzled too. I had the feeling of victory again, the same feeling I had at the party the first night in Dallas. What were a few doubts compared to the reality of a beautiful, begging Beth Ann Deering. You believe what you want to believe.

16

Tony thought that the word *police* had "a nice ring to it." In fact, when I returned from the Deering's, everyone gave a little cheer as if to celebrate that I came back alive.

While I was gone, plans had been made about how to spend the afternoon. Everyone had a say but me. It was agreed that we would drive around Dallas and see the city. If anyone had asked, I would have been the first to agree, because I hadn't really seen the place. Last night in Delphine's car hardly counted. Mia and Heidi had a good tour in Delphine's car but Heidi said it didn't count, because it was "store-oriented." The maid promised Mia that she would faithfully answer all phone calls. So, the seven of us were off on our great adventure in Tony's Mercedes.

The parts of the city that he drove us through were bright, modern, busy, and full of tall buildings. "Where are the Dallas Cowboys?" Heidi asked. She didn't care about football, but she wanted to tell the kids back home that she had seen them.

"They're not walking down the street, dear," Jewel said. "Although one never knows."

"Where's Neiman-Marcus?" Mom asked.

"You'll see it. Never fear," said Tony.

"I want to see the fancy hotel with those elevators on the outside," Heidi requested.

"Tell you what," said Jewel. "How would you like to take an elevator that gives you a view of the outside while you're going up, and when you reach the top you can have lunch there."

"You have lunch at the top of the elevator?" I laughed. "I bet it's not crowded there. Anyway, forget elevators and lunch. I want to see where the *Dallas* TV show is filmed."

"Requests, requests," Jewel said, putting her hand over her ears. But I knew she loved these requests. This was the biggest party of them all—showing us Dallas. I wished I had brought my tape recorder to record my impressions. I had begun to carry it in my pocket wherever I went. But I changed into what my mother called "city clothes" just before we left the house, and I forgot to transfer my recorder.

It didn't much matter. We finally drove by the TV *Dallas* house, and it wasn't any big deal.

"It's just like on TV," Heidi said. She seemed thrilled and disappointed at the same time. What did she expect?

"So long, Southfork," she said. "What's next?"

"We have a new Museum of Fine Arts," Tony said.

I groaned.

I think we would have toured into the night, but I had to get back to go to the party Beth Ann begged me to attend. When we got home I went to my room and pulled my tape recorder out of my jeans pocket. I didn't want it to land up in the laundry. Besides, I had to tell it about my visit to Beth Ann's house.

I pressed the record button. *"This morning I went to Beth Ann's house and—"*

"Ted!" Mia was standing at the door to my room. "Who are you talking to, Ted?"

I stuck the recorder in my pocket. "Nobody. Nobody."

"Look, I heard you. It's okay, Ted."

"What's okay? What do you mean? You've got that big-sister look on your face again. You're getting ready to give me another lecture."

"No. By now *you*, little brother, should have figured out Beth Ann and Delphine. I mean, you *are* suspicious. That business about telling Delphine you're fifteen and the way she shrugged it off."

"Wait a minute. How do you know about that?"

How *did* Mia know about the fifteen business? Oh no! Say it isn't so! She couldn't have—did she?

"I heard your tape, Ted."

"You've been eavesdropping. How can you put down Delphine and Beth Ann when you do something like this?"

How much did Mia hear?

She walked into the room. She was mad. "Ted, you know me better than that. I would never eavesdrop. Jewel gave me a tape recorder this morning while you were at Beth Ann's. She gave one to Heidi, too.

92

She said that you have one, and therefore Heidi and I should each have one. But she ran out of tapes. She said you had plenty."

I looked at the top of my dresser. Tapes were all over it. Unused tapes. No, *one* of them was used. Why hadn't I put it in the drawer?

Mia kept on talking. "Jewel gave us a couple of your tapes from the top of your dresser. She figured you hadn't used them yet. You've got such a big collection. She gave one to me and one to Heidi. I tried mine by myself. I was going to record our tour of the city and play it for Kristi when I got back to Phoenix. I've been sending her postcards, but this would be a real treat. Anyway, I was practicing, fooling around with the buttons. Forward, rewind, play, stop. Just getting acquainted with the little cassette. Suddenly I heard your voice. I heard what you said about Delphine."

"Did you hear anything else?"

"No."

"Did you tell anybody?"

"Oh, c'mon, Ted. I put the tape right back on your dresser."

"Sorry."

Mia didn't move.

"I said I was sorry."

"Apology accepted. But what about—"

"I'm handling things now. Trust me."

I don't know what Mia would have answered. The telephone rang. Mia stops in her tracks when the telephone rings. She was already stopped in her tracks, so she stayed there.

Jewel yelled, "Mia! Telephone!"

Mia left the room like a shot. I hoped it was Neal calling. Should I tell Mia that the tape recorder would be great for confiding her thoughts about Neal? No, she didn't need it.

I went to the head of the stairs. I heard Mia kind of shriek, "Neal!"

I was glad for Mia.

I went back to my room. I had to get ready for the party. But what about my used tapes? Where would be a good place to hide them? Maybe I should erase them. If I couldn't store information in my head, maybe it wasn't worth storing. Still, I might be erasing pure gold. Couldn't do that.

I stuck the tapes in my sneakers. Not the ones I planned to wear.

17

The party took place in a house a couple of blocks away. It was in honor of a guy named Jason, who had just moved on the block with his family. All the guests looked like teen-agers including a girl named Sally, who kept giving me the eye. But I already had enough trouble with friendly girls. Most of the other girls were paying attention to Jason. I realized that he had two things going for him. He was new, and he was permanent.

Delphine showed up about ten minutes after Beth Ann and I arrived at the party. She waved to me, but she didn't come over. Probably because I was with Beth Ann. That's what I thought, until I saw Delphine rush up to Jason. He was standing in the middle of the living room. He already had a little circle of girls around him. I compared myself to Jason. He looked like a surfer, like he was imported from California intact with beach, ocean and suntan lotion as part of his body equipment. I found out later that he was from Michigan and he hated anything connected with water. He was an intellectual. At only sixteen. Sometimes intellectuals aren't smart, they're just intelligent. Jason was smart. I didn't know that immediately though.

Delphine kind of elbowed some girls and managed to get next to Jason. Beth Ann said to me, "I'll be back," and she did a repeat of Delphine's actions. They were standing side by side gazing up at Jason. I felt abandoned.

I moved closer to Jason, too. I wanted to see what was going on. I wished I had my recorder with me. Maybe I could have taped everything secretly and then played it back privately. I could pick up knowledge that might be useful to me for the rest of my natural life. I had become an *observer*. When you stand back and watch and listen, something clicks in you that does not click when you're part of the action. I hoped I would remember to tell that sentence to my recorder. It sounded wise and it might even be accurate.

"Are you Jason?"

Delphine was talking to the intellectual who looked like a surfer.

Jason nodded yes.

Beth Ann spoke up. "Of course he's Jason. Can't you tell?"

Something sounded familiar. Hadn't Delphine and Beth Ann greeted me the same way the first night I was in Dallas? Yes, I was sure of it!

"Welcome to Dallas," Delphine said. "I'm Delphine Rasmussen."

"And I'm Beth Ann Deering," said Beth Ann. "A friend of Delphine's."

Why were Delphine and Beth Ann always declaring their friendship? Especially since that was the *only* way it seemed to exist—through a declaration; it did not exist in fact. Looking at them, I, Ted, the observer, knew for sure that basically the two girls were serious competitors—rivals. They thrived on it. I had suspected, but now I was positive. O tape recorder, mark this well: Delphine Rasmussen and Beth Ann Deering are rivals, and I was for a brief moment in time the object of their rivalry. I might even go so far as to say their sex object, but they never really tried anything.

Jason was looking the girls over. "Nice to meet you," he said.

"Have you gotten acquainted with our city yet?" Beth Ann asked.

"A bit," said Jason.

"What haven't you seen?" Delphine asked. "I'd be glad to show you around. I'm known for my tours."

Beth Ann kind of glared at Delphine. But she said to her sweetly, "Doesn't your mom ever get tired of being the tour guide?"

Jason was smiling. These girls were after him, and he knew it. I felt like slinking away. I knew the truth now. I had only been part of their usual routine—a new guy to compete for. Not a person, just a new guy. No wonder they never cared whether I exaggerated or told the truth. How could I have been so stupid? I knew. I hoped I could remember this for the tape recorder: when you're flattered, you're automatically stupid. The two go together.

Now that I was out of it, really out of it, I decided to hang around and try to enjoy the show. I was already rejected. I had nothing to lose. I learned my lesson. I'd be a wiser person back in Arizona.

Beth Ann was asking Jason, "What's it like where you come from?"

I was completely surprised when I heard Jason answer with magical words: *"Excuse me."* He walked out of the room and went outside to the pool area. He was escaping from Beth Ann and Delphine! What class! He was rejecting them!

I wished I could go back to my first evening in Dallas. At the party. I wished I would have had the brains to say, "Excuse me" and then walk away from Delphine and Beth Ann. I would give those words the delivery they deserved. Maybe I'd say them like a Shakespearean actor or an Academy Award winner or something. *"Excuse me."* It would roll off my tongue perfectly. But my chance was gone.

Delphine and Beth Ann were now looking at each other. They shrugged their shoulders as if to say Oh well. I wondered if they'd try again with Jason or just give up. Maybe they'd go looking for another prize at the party. But they came over to me.

"Sorry to have rushed off, Ted," Beth Ann said. "Delphine and I just wanted to make Jason feel welcome in Dallas."

"Yeah, I guess you two are kind of a Welcome Wagon team."

They both smiled vacantly. "Want to go sit by the pool?" Beth Ann asked.

"No thanks. I've been sitting in a car most of the afternoon."

"You could stand by the pool," Delphine offered. "There's food out there, too."

"Okay," I said, suddenly changing my mind.

I was interested in seeing what would happen outside. Jason was talking to a pretty red-haired girl. I could see them through the window. The pool and the patio were all lit up.

The three of us went outside. Delphine instantly went up to Jason and asked if he'd like "some Texas refreshments."

"Not hungry, thanks," he said, and he went on talking to the other girl.

Not hungry. I'd have to tell those words to my recorder. They were symbolic. Not hungry as in not hungry for attention, not hungry for girls fawning over you. Jason was one cool guy.

I took some food. No one had offered to get me any. Delphine and Beth Ann were standing off to the side, talking to each other. I ate like a pig. I had a wonderful appetite. Maybe that's a sign of being reborn.

I decided to leave the party. Why stay? I had eaten, I had gotten an education—what else was there to do? The girl named Sally was still eyeing me, but I wasn't in the mood for girls. I was in the mood for cars, for my tape recorder, for my family, for everything that was familiar, that didn't have to be figured out.

I turned to leave. I walked away from the pool.

"Stop! Where are you going, Ted?"

Beth Ann was calling after me.

"Home," I said without turning around.

"But we've only been here a little while," she said. "You're my date and I'm your date. We stick together."

"That's news to me," I said. "You two are too much."

Delphine came up and took my arm. "Oh, Teddy, what would the party be without you."

"Exactly the same," I said, freeing my arm. I looked at the two girls. I knew I could have them back for the evening, maybe for the rest of my vacation. I could play a game with them, too, if I wanted to. I didn't.

"*Excuse me,*" I said. I said it twice. I didn't do it justice the first time.

I left the party. I left Beth Ann. I left Delphine. I left part of my ego. I didn't want that part anymore. The part that could get fooled. I hoped that it would stay forever in Dallas, Texas.

18

"Where has the vacation gone?" Mom asked Jewel.

"That question means you had a good time," Jewel answered.

Mom and Jewel were sitting on the patio. Jewel was drinking her seventh cup of coffee of the morning, and Mom was stretched out in total relaxation. They were like two kittens, each comfortable under the sun in her own style.

It was our last full day in Dallas. Our vacation seemed to go by faster and faster the past few days. We did more sightseeing. Randy and his parents had all of us over for dinner. Jewel bought Mia some real cowboy boots to wear for her reunion with Neal, whenever that was. Heidi had been invited to swim in almost every pool in the area. She claimed to be famous throughout several thousand acres.

I liked the last part of our stay in Dallas better than the first. I didn't have Delphine or Beth Ann on the brain anymore. I could relax. Also, I had become a hero of sorts with Jewel and Tony. We had not heard one bark, woof, whine or yelp from the Deerings' dog since I had my getting-tough talk with Beth Ann about Duke.

Did that mean that Beth Ann respected me? Maybe she did. Maybe she and Delphine came to realize that they couldn't take advantage of me anymore. But I had my doubts. I could have been a good sport and called them to say goodbye, but why bother to say goodbye to people you wished you had never said hello to.

I *did* owe one phone call. It nagged at me. I had never called Laura Erskine-Chamberlin again. I felt so deflated after my experience with Delphine and Beth Ann that I decided to forget Dallas girls. Back in Phoenix I could start fresh and new.

But I had promised Laura I'd call back. What if she was waiting for my call? I didn't want her to think of me the way I thought about Delphine and Beth Ann. I wanted her to continue thinking of me as a nice guy.

I got my tape recorder. I was now hiding my used tapes in a soap dish in my drawer. They fitted like they were made to lie in that soap dish. But it could only hold two tapes. I was making my recordings more brief. I told my recorder: *"Dana Andrews is about to call Gene Tierney. If this is a mistake, speak now or forever hold your silence."*

I couldn't find Laura's telephone number. So much for that. I wasn't supposed to call her. Otherwise I wouldn't have lost her telephone number.

I found it. Under a tape.

I dialed Laura's number.

I hoped she wasn't home.

"Hello."

"Hi, it's me, Dana Andrews."

For someone who hoped Laura wasn't home, I was sure into the spirit of things.

"Dana! I thought you had disappeared. What's new? How's your friend? Did he decide on which girl he likes?"

"He decided he didn't like either one of them. He peeled away their surface and he found plastic and gloss and junk like that."

"Did you help him make the discovery?"

"Sure. I was right there."

"Does he feel bad?"

"Not any more. Everything's an experience, right?"

"Right. So when are you going back to Phoenix? Isn't it almost time?"

"Tomorrow afternoon. I leave tomorrow afternoon."

"That's almost here."

"Yuh, almost here." Did I sigh? I felt a little sad.

"I guess I won't be meeting you—that is, in person."

"Well, there's still a chance." I wanted there to be a chance. It seemed like Dallas wasn't complete without my meeting Laura. "I can meet you tonight, Laura."

I said it. I came right out and told her I'd meet her. No more fudging, no more excuses. At last I was available.

"I can't meet you tonight, Dana."

She can't meet *me?* She had a sense of humor, that's what she had.

I laughed. "I bet that's a line from the movie. Like Miss Gene is playing hard to get, putting Dana off, but she's just teasing. Does it come early in the picture or later? I'll watch for it."

"I've got a date tonight, Ted. Honestly."

She wasn't kidding. I could tell the way she said it. She was trying to be nice. I felt like a jerk for thinking she'd be available whenever I was. Now I'd never meet her.

"I know this was kind of a last-minute invitation," I said. "But in a way, this is my last minute in Dallas. I mean, it's my last night tonight."

"I'm sorry. I really wish I could have met you."

"So do I."

I was thinking of all the time I had spent with Beth Ann and Delphine that I could have spent with Laura. Every time I spoke to Laura she sounded more and more like a great person. It was my fault that I had never met her.

"Well," I said, "it was nice talking to you over the phone. I enjoyed it."

"Me, too. I hope you have a wonderful trip back to Arizona."

"Thanks. Well goodbye."

"Goodbye."

I went back outside. Mia was sitting alone by the pool.

"Where's everybody?" I asked.

"Heidi's at a neighbor's pool, and everybody else is

getting ready to go shopping. It was Mom's idea, not Jewel's. How about that? She and Dad want to buy some presents for Tony and Jewel. Mom wants them to pick the presents themselves so they'll have a chance to get something they really want."

"I think they've got everything they want."

"They'll discover something else. After all the gifts they gave us, I hope they end up with something terrific."

"Aren't you going with them?"

"No, I've got too much packing to do. I threw out a bunch of my old ratty stuff, but I picked up lots of new things, thanks to Jewel. She bought them for me. She says I should have new stuff to wear the next time I see Neal." Mia pointed to the chair beside her. "Sit down, little brother."

"Don't you have to pack?"

"Plenty of time. You look depressed. Is it okay to tell you that? I don't want to butt in again."

"You're not."

"I never forgot how you tried to help me when I had a problem with Neal. Remember the coffee pot incident? I owe you."

"No you don't."

"You got a problem now, Ted? Tell me to be quiet and I will."

"It's not a problem. It's a let-down feeling. Like I blew a situation. I wasted time on Delphine and Beth Ann, and I never got to meet Laura Erskine-Chamberlin. I kept putting her off, and now it's too late. I just called her, and she's busy tonight."

"Rotten luck. But maybe Delphine and Beth Ann

weren't a total waste of time. Everything's an experience. This whole trip was a learning experience, wasn't it, Ted? Dealing with new people, new places. I feel years older than when we started."

"You *talk* years older. Learning experience, all that stuff. You've changed places with Mom and Dad. They seem years younger. Sometimes they act like kids."

"Yeah, isn't it nice? Maybe they've learned how to do that. I'm glad we took this vacation together, all of us. I even got to know *you* better."

The conversation was getting sticky. I had gotten to know Mia better. She had become someone I could count on as a friend. But it was hard to come out and say that.

"Everything's okay, pal," I said. She knew what I meant.

Mia got up. "Guess I'll pack. See you later—pal." She kissed me on the cheek and walked off. I felt better. I went to my room and started to pack. I picked up my tape recorder. Should I tell it what had happened with Beth Ann and Delphine and Laura? No. I knew what happened with the girls. And for the first time since I got to Dallas, that seemed to be enough.

I kept looking at the recorder. It had become an old friend—the kind of friend that doesn't carry tales and really knows how to listen. I put it in my pocket. Aunt Jewel had given it to me, and I was glad to have it. I was going to keep it. After all, I could always benefit from having a good listener around.

19

I was alone in the house. We had all gone out for "a last Dallas dinner" and come back stuffed with mesquite broiled T-bone steaks. Jewel had suggested a long stroll around the neighborhood to walk off our dinners. But I wanted to examine our car and make sure it was ready for our trip tomorrow. Dad had already had it checked out at a gas station, but one of the tires didn't look right to me.

I changed into my worst clothes. Mia had thrown away her ratty things, but I liked my old clothes. Most of them were already packed for the trip home. I had just put on my grease-stained T-shirt when the doorbell rang.

By now I knew that the maid did not answer doorbells. I did. I opened the door. Then I nearly fell over. Delphine and Beth Ann were standing there!

"Hi, Ted," Delphine said. "Do you mind a couple of visitors?"

I looked down at my grease-stained shirt. I hoped that the girls found it disgusting. "Come in," I said.

They came in and sat down on a sofa. I sat down on a chair across from them. I waited. It was up to them to talk first.

"We came to say goodbye," Beth Ann said. "We're going to miss you, Ted."

"Sure," I said. "You're gonna cry your eyes out."

"We mean it," said Delphine.

"Sure," I said again.

What were they after now? I was leaving Dallas. It was too late for them to score points.

"Don't be angry at us, Ted," Delphine went on. "We always liked you."

She was giving me the same look she gave me when I first met her. She should save it for another novice, not waste it on a veteran like me.

"Delphine and I have just a little problem," Beth Ann said, picking up where Delphine had left off. "Everything seems to be a challenge. Everybody seems to be a challenge."

"A game is more like it," I said.

"Okay," said Beth Ann. "And we kind of get caught up in it. We can't help ourselves. But you caught on, Ted."

Delphine fluffed her hair. "Some guys like it. They don't care whether we mean it or not. They enjoy the attention anyway. You're more—serious. But we didn't know that. When you told us all those wild, extravagant stories at the party, well, why should we have taken you seriously?"

She was dead right.

Beth Ann smiled. "*You* were a pretty good game player, Ted, but you pooped out."

"I was always just an amateur," I said. "And I've quit permanently."

"Maybe we'll quit," Delphine said.

"Don't be drastic, Delphine," said Beth Ann. "We'll take each situation one at a time."

"But we both really like you, Ted," said Delphine. "Think about it. We didn't have to come and tell you."

I wished that Mia were there. I needed her opinion. Were these girls finally being honest with me? I wanted to believe them, because it was a nice deal for my ego—to be liked, admired, by these two beautiful girls.

Beth Ann added three more words. "We're sorry, Ted."

That did it. I believed them. I even understood them.

It was my turn to say something nice to these girls. I couldn't just accept their compliments without giving something back. But no games. I couldn't tell them anything that wasn't true.

"You girls," I said, "you girls are fun. You'll be a part of my memory of Dallas as a place to have a good time."

I guess I could have described an amusement park the same way. But Beth Ann grinned, stood up, came over to where I was sitting, kissed me right on the mouth and said, "You're so cute, Ted."

Then Delphine did exactly the same thing.

I'll never know whether they meant those kisses, but I was glad to have them anyway.

They walked toward the door. I grabbed their hands. "Thanks for coming over," I said.

"Drop us a card from Phoenix, Ted," Delphine said. "And call us if you ever get back to Dallas."

"Have a good trip, Ted," Beth Ann said.

I let go of their hands and they were out the door.

20

The next morning I went next door and said goodbye to Randy. I almost felt like his equal in maturity.
I knew I wasn't, but I felt that way that morning. I
told him I hoped he'd still be living next door to Jewel
and Tony the next time I visited Dallas. I gave him my
address in case he ever got to Phoenix. We didn't
promise to write to each other, because guys don't
usually keep that kind of promise. Anyway, I knew I
was still a teen-age kid in his eyes. And let's face it, in
fact, too.

We were sitting by Randy's pool when Jewel came
running over. "Telephone, Ted," she said.

Randy smiled. "Go to it, Ted." He must have figured
that a girl was calling me.

"See ya," I said. "Goodbye." I ran back to the house
with Jewel. Who would be calling me? It was probably Delphine and Beth Ann, cementing all the good

feelings of the night before. I didn't want to ask Jewel if it really was a girl on the line.

At the house she said, "You can take it in your room. And I'll hang up down here."

I went up to my room, picked up the receiver, said Hello, and Jewel clicked off. I was alone with whoever was calling.

"Hi, Dana."

"Laura!" I couldn't believe how happy I was to hear from her.

"Listen, Dana. I called to invite you to breakfast or brunch, wherever your stomach is at."

"You mean right now?"

"Sure. It just dawned on me that we could still meet. You said you weren't leaving until this afternoon. But if you're busy packing or something—"

"No. Not busy."

We were going to meet after all! But what if I was disappointed? What if Laura was disappointed? There was something depressing but very romantic about never having met.

"Wonderful," she was saying. "How about coming in fifteen minutes?"

"Okay. Where do you live?"

"Doesn't matter. Jewel will drive you."

She knew Jewel. Of course.

When I got off the phone and I told Jewel and my mother where I was going, Jewel practically pushed me into the car. I protested. "She said fifteen minutes, Jewel. Where does she live, two minutes from here?"

"So? Surprise her. Be a bit early. Do it with flair, Ted." Jewel pinched my cheek and slammed the car door shut. As we drove along she said, "Do you know what a triumph this is for me, my dear nephew? I've been trying desperately to get the two of you together. And this is so dramatic. The last day of your vacation. It will be something marvelous to tell to your tape-recorder friend back in Phoenix."

Jewel pulled up in front of a nice-looking but plain kind of house. "Could we just drive around the block a couple of times?" I asked. "So I won't be too early."

"Remember flair," Jewel said. Then she practically pushed me out of the car. "You'll probably get a ride home. But if not, just give me a buzz. Have a good time, Ted. I'm so happy!"

I went up the front walk. I realized suddenly that Laura's mother had been the first to arrive at Jewel's house the day I met her. Maybe their family believed in early arrivals. I also remembered that she had seen my glistening body that day. Had she told Laura about that? Would she once again refer to me as a hunk? I hoped *she* didn't have a crush on me or something. The guys back in Phoenix liked to kid about older women and younger men and said the movie makers made a lot of bucks on this idea. I personally didn't want any mother-daughter combination fighting over me.

Laura's mother opened the door, but she didn't seem to recognize me. It was mildly deflating—but only temporary. "Oh yes," she said as if she were talking to herself, "Jewel's nephew. The exercise person from Phoenix."

I hadn't said a word. All I had done was smile when she opened the door.

"Laura said she was expecting a friend," Mrs. Erskine-Chamberlin continued. "Do come in. Laura's on the side patio putting the finishing touches on brunch."

Mrs. Erskine-Chamberlin led me through the house. There was something circular about it. It looked more complicated than it had seemed from the street. She slid open a glass door and said, "Laura's out there." Then she left.

I saw a slim, almost skinny girl, standing over a table, putting some spoons and forks in place. Her back was toward me.

"Laura?"

"Dana," she said, without turning around. Obviously she had a talent for the dramatic. One hundred girls out of one hundred would have turned around immediately.

I walked up to her and stood beside her. Then she turned. A second before she turned I knew that I didn't care what she looked like. I was already attracted to her.

She was ordinary-looking in an old-fashioned kind of way. Her brown hair hung down like it was a victim of the humidity. Most of the girls I knew didn't allow their hair to be victims of the humidity. What they did about it, I don't know, but it worked. Laura had gray-colored eyes, and her face had a clean glow. I was glad that I met her after the dazzle of Beth Ann and Delphine had faded. I was ready to appreciate Laura Erskine-Chamberlin.

"At last," she said.

"At last."

What did she think of *me*? It would help if she had had a rotten experience on her date the night before so that she would be in the mood to appreciate me. Not that I wished her a truly rotten experience. Maybe just total boredom from beginning to end.

I couldn't tell what she thought of me. She said, "Sit down. Everything's set. Cold stuff, hot stuff. The hot stuff's in the covered keep-warm dishes."

I sat down. The table looked nice. I was glad to see there wasn't any gold silverware. No maid was around to serve either.

"My parents already ate," Laura said. "So all of this is for us."

There were strawberries and melons, a pitcher of orange juice, a pitcher of milk, a pot of coffee, cream, sugar, jams, marmalade. Laura lifted the covers of the keep-warm dishes. "For your inspection," she said, laughing. The first dish contained scrambled eggs. Thin pancakes were in another. Then sausages! And fried potatoes! Laura kept lifting. I kept inspecting. Then I lifted three covers myself. I found toast, hot rolls, and blueberry muffins. It looked great, but did she do all this just for me?

I was curious. "Do you ever just grab a bowl of cold cereal in the morning and call it quits?"

"Cold cereal? Want some?"

"No, I already had some today."

"If that's all you had, then you're hungry. Dig in."

I dug in. There was a breeze going across the patio. There were tall trees shading us from the sun, and pots of bright flowers everywhere. Great place. I couldn't see a pool from where I was sitting. Maybe

115

there was one in back of the house.

I had a lot to talk about, but I found myself heading in one direction.

"How was your date last night?" I asked between bites of strawberries. I didn't think Laura would mind a direct question.

"Okay."

"Okay as in boring?"

I was being too direct. I knew it the minute I asked. Laura coolly ate some strawberries. "Okay as in okay," she said. Then she added, "I'm not as experienced as you about dates—knowing about the opposite sex, like you do, and giving advice like you do. That's a heavy load, isn't it?"

"It's lighter than you'd think."

I didn't want to go into how light it was. I changed the subject. "Say, these are very good strawberries."

"It must be wonderful to be sophisticated and sure of yourself," she continued.

I could see that she was giving me a chance to talk about myself. After all, I had already made a big impression over the phone. But this could be much bigger. She was really asking for it.

"Do you grow your own strawberries?" I asked.

"No. I'm so glad you found time in your busy schedule to come over here and meet me."

This was opportunity, no doubt about it. I could tell her anything, and she'd believe it. But I didn't want to. Last week I would have done it. Face it, last week I *did* it. But no more. Total honesty was Ted Fisher's new policy.

"I understand reality," Laura said.

"You do?"

"Yes. You didn't want to meet me because you had better things to do. But I was willing to be put off. I didn't mind."

"Oh, good."

"I do favors for my mother all the time. She's always lining up blind dates for me. Usually they turn out to be turkeys."

"Huh?" *I* was a favor she did for her *mother*?

"Sometimes I think Mom collects all the turkeys in the barnyard and turns them over to me. I'm glad you're not a turkey."

"Thanks for the compliment."

What compliment? I had gotten better ones the night before from Delphine and Beth Ann. And I didn't have to leave the house to get them. I scooped out some eggs from the keep-warm dish and dumped them on my plate while I tried to figure out what was happening. Laura had been almost fawning over me and then, I found myself thanking her for not thinking I was a turkey. I was insulted. I was fascinated.

Laura took some eggs, too. "Maybe you can give me some advice," she said.

"You don't need any."

"What?"

The eggs must have cleared my head. "You don't want advice from me," I said. "You're putting me on. Admit it."

Laura hesitated. Then she said, "Okay, I am. You deserved it. You kept telling me over the phone that you were giving advice. But I could tell that *you* were the one who needed it. That's why I gave you a little."

"You knew the advice was for *me?*"

"Of course. I was waiting for you to admit it. But you kept getting in deeper. I guess it was too hard to turn back. Have some more eggs."

"Why did you invite me to brunch?"

"I wanted to meet Dana."

"I'm not Dana."

"To me you are. You're okay. You were so unreal about what you were telling me over the phone that I realized that basically you must be a very honest person or you wouldn't be so bad at being dishonest."

"I didn't make up those two girls—"

"Maybe not. But you weren't any hotshot lady-killer who should be giving advice."

I stood up. "Thanks for the strawberries and the eggs."

Laura put her hand on my arm. "Sit down. You weren't listening. I said you're okay. Am I okay?"

"You're asking me?"

"Yes. Should I have told you right from the start that I didn't believe you? I want your opinion of me."

"Boy, you're direct."

"I know it. Is that a fault? Tell me your opinion."

"My opinion is that you should have told me right from the start that you didn't believe me."

"Good. We're having an honest conversation. But you didn't tell me what you think of me."

"You're interesting."

"Interesting enough to remember when you get back to Phoenix?"

"I'll remember you."

Laura put a blueberry muffin on my plate. "I have a friend from camp who lives near Phoenix. Sometimes I visit her."

"Is that a hint?"

"You bet."

"You want to see me again? That's what you're telling me?" *I wanted to see her, too!*

"Sure. And I'll write to you in the meantime if I know you'll answer."

"I hate to write letters."

I was so happy I was stupid. I hadn't meant to say that.

Laura looked at me. She seemed hurt.

I said quickly, "I didn't mean it that way. I meant to say that there's an easier way to communicate. Do you own a tape recorder?"

"Sure. Ah! Sending tapes. That's what you mean. Great idea."

"Isn't it? Nobody writes letters anymore. I have it on good authority."

21

The saddest part of our entire vacation was saying goodbye to Jewel and Tony.

Heidi was just about crying. "You have to visit us in Phoenix," she said. "We'll be home next week. You could take a plane and even meet us at our door when we get there. Oh, please. Say you'll do it."

"Oh, Heidi," Jewel said, hugging her. "We'll come soon, I promise."

"You could come in the car with us right now, you and Tony," Heidi said. "Not our car. We could sell that and take one of yours and Tony's and we could all travel together just like we did when we drove around Dallas."

"We can't right now," Tony said, "but we sure will visit you, pardner. That's a promise."

Tony was wearing his new ten-gallon cowboy hat. My parents had bought it for him. Jewel had bought one for me. Tony gave a little salute to Heidi by touching his hat. I wondered how I'd look if I tried that with my hat.

Heidi wasn't the only one about to cry. Mom was on the verge. She said, "It seems as if we just got here."

"You did," said Jewel. "This wasn't a long stay, Gwen. Next time plan for the entire summer."

It seemed like the family was splitting up. The five Fishers had become a very close group on our trip to Dallas, and then in Dallas, Jewel and Tony had kind of merged with us, and we became a family of seven. Now the five of us were separating from Jewel and Tony, and it was sad. But people live where they have to live, and sometimes that means families are far apart. In a year Mia would be going off to college, and only four of us would be left at home.

At last we piled into the car. The same positions as before. Mom and Dad up front. Mia in the middle in the back seat, with Heidi on one side of her and me on the other. It used to be a drag but it seemed to be a family tradition now that nobody wanted to break.

Dad started the car and we drove off, waving like crazy to Jewel and Tony, who were waving like crazy. I realized I was also leaving Delphine and Beth Ann, Laura, Randy, and the city of Dallas, and Duke the dog and things that mattered and things that didn't. They were all bunched together in my head. In my pocket was my address book with the names and addresses of the three girls. Delphine and Beth Ann would each get one postcard from me. Laura would get a long tape.

Jewel had insisted on making reservations for us to

spend the night at a fancy motel about two hundred and fifty miles west of Dallas. After we had driven for about half an hour, Heidi asked, "Are we there yet?"

"Not quite," Mom answered, smiling.

I reached up and touched my hat—the way Tony had touched his when he saluted Heidi. I'd have to practice that touch. I sat back and felt a light thud. The tape recorder moved in my pocket. I wondered if I had a clean tape to use for Laura. It wasn't a problem I had to worry about; I could just record over my old tapes. No, I couldn't do that, I had to keep them. And update them. I wanted to have a permanent record of Ted Fisher's User's Manual on Girls.

We were definitely on the road again. I leaned over to Heidi. "Don't worry, Heidi," I said. "Maybe we're not there yet, but I think the Fisher family has come a long, long way."

Marjorie Sharmat

<u>knows</u> about falling in love!

___HE NOTICED I'M ALIVE...
    AND OTHER HOPEFUL SIGNS
                93809-0 $2.25

___HOW TO HAVE A GORGEOUS
    WEDDING   93794-9 $2.95

___HOW TO MEET A GORGEOUS
    GIRL   93808-2 $2.95

___HOW TO MEET A GORGEOUS
    GUY   93553-9 $2.95

___I SAW HIM FIRST
                94009-5 $2.95

___TWO GUYS NOTICED
    ME...AND OTHER MIRACLES
            98846-2 $2.95

You'll find a friend in these bestsellers by

Judy Blume

___ARE YOU THERE GOD? IT'S ME, MARGARET....	90419-6	$2.95
___BLUBBER	90707-1	$2.95
___DEENIE	93259-9	$3.25
___IT'S NOT THE END OF THE WORLD	94140-7	$3.25
___STARRING SALLY J. FREEDMAN	98239-1	$3.25
___THEN AGAIN MAYBE I WON'T	98659-1	$2.95
___TIGER EYES	98469-6	$3.25